The Coming of the Fairies

SIR ARTHUR
CONAN DOYLE

This edition published in Great Britain in 1997 by Pavilion Books Limited
London House
Great Eastern Wharf
Parkgate Road
London
SW11 4NQ

Originally published in 1922 by Hodder and Stoughton

Copyright © 1996 Sheldon Reynolds.
Administrator of the Conan Doyle Copyrights
Photographs: 24, 30, 55, 59, 61 © University of Leeds Library,
Brotherton Collection; 34, 38, 49, 66, 70, 93 © Reproduced by permission
of The British Library from the 1922 edition of *The Coming of the Fairies*,
shelfmark 8833.b.16.

A CIP catalogue record for this book is available from the British Library

ISBN 1 86205 122 4

Typeset in 11/13 Bembo by Textype, England
Printed and bound in Great Britain by
Caledonian International Book Manufacturing Ltd, Glasgow

3 5 7 9 8 6 4

This book may be ordered by post direct from the publisher.
Please contact the Marketing Department. But try your bookshop first,

Preface

This book contains reproductions of the famous Cottingley photographs, and gives the whole of the evidence in connection with them. The diligent reader is in almost as good a position as I am to form a judgment upon the authenticity of the pictures. This narrative is not a special plea for that authenticity, but is simply a collection of facts the inferences from which may be accepted or rejected as the reader may think fit.

I would warn the critic, however, not to be led away by the sophistry that because some professional trickster, apt at the game of deception, can produce a somewhat similar effect, therefore the originals were produced in the same way. There are few realities which cannot be imitated, and the ancient argument that because conjurers on their own prepared plates or stages can produce certain results, therefore similar results obtained by untrained people under natural conditions are also false, is surely discounted by the intelligent public.

I would add that this whole subject of the objective existence of a subhuman form of life has nothing to do with the larger and far more vital question of spiritualism. I should be sorry if my arguments in favour of the latter should be in any way weakened by my exposition of this very strange episode, which has really no bearing upon the continued existence of the individual.

ARTHUR CONAN DOYLE
CROWBOROUGH
March 1922.

Contents

Illustrations

———

CHAPTER I

How the Matter Arose

The series of incidents set forth in this little volume represent either the most elaborate and ingenious hoax ever played upon the public, or else they constitute an event in human history which may in the future appear to have been epoch-making in its character. It is hard for the mind to grasp what the ultimate results may be if we have actually proved the existence upon the surface of this planet of a population which may be as numerous as the human race, which pursues its own strange life in its own strange way, and which is only separated from ourselves by some difference of vibrations. We see objects within the limits which make up our colour spectrum, with infinite vibrations, unused by us, on either side of them. If we could conceive a race of beings which were constructed in material which threw out shorter or longer vibrations, they would be invisible unless we could tune ourselves up or tone them down. It is exactly that power of tuning up and adapting itself to other vibrations which constitutes a clairvoyant, and there is nothing scientifically impossible, so far as I can see, in some people seeing that which is invisible to others. If the objects are indeed there, and if the inventive power of the human brain is turned upon the problem, it is likely that some sort of psychic spectacles, inconceivable to us at the moment, will be invented, and that we shall all be able to adapt ourselves to the new conditions. If high-tension electricity can be converted by a mechanical contrivance into a lower tension, keyed to other uses, then it is hard to see why something analogous might not occur with the vibrations of ether and the waves of light.

This, however, is mere speculation and leads me to the fact that early in May 1920 I heard, in conversation with my friend Mr. Gow, the Editor of *Light*, that alleged photographs of fairies had been taken. He had not actually seen them, but he referred me to Miss Scatcherd, a lady for whose knowledge and judgment I had considerable respect. I got into touch with her and found that she also had not seen the photographs, but she had a friend, Miss Gardner, who had actually done so. On May 13 Miss Scatcherd wrote to me saying that she was getting on the trail, and including an extract from a letter of Miss Gardner, which ran as follows. I am quoting actual documents in this early stage, for I think there are many who would like a complete inside view of all that led up to so remarkable an episode. Alluding to her brother Mr. Gardner, she says:

"You know that Edward is a Theosophist, has been for years, and now he is mostly engaged with lecturing and other work for the Society—and although for years I have regarded him as bathed in error and almost past praying for, I now find a talk with him an inspiring privilege. I am so very thankful that I happened to be in Willesden when his bereavement took place, for it was so wonderful to watch him, and to see how marvellously his faith and beliefs upheld and comforted him. He will probably devote more and more of his time and strength to going about the country lecturing, etc.

"I wish you could see a photo he has. He believes in fairies, pixies, goblins, etc.—children, in many cases, really see them and play with them. He has got into touch with a family in Bradford where the little girl, Elsie, and her cousin, Frances, constantly go into woods and play with the fairies. The father and mother are sceptical and have no sympathy with their nonsense, as they call it, but an aunt, whom Edward has interviewed, is quite sympathetic with the girls. Some little time ago, Elsie said she wanted to photograph them, and begged her father to lend his camera. For long he refused, but at last she managed to get the loan of it and one plate. Off she and Frances went into the woods near a waterfall. Frances ' 'ticed' them, as they call it, and Elsie stood ready with the camera. Soon the three fairies appeared, and one pixie dancing in Frances' aura. Elsie snapped and hoped for the best. It was a long time before the father would develop the photo, but at last he did, and to his utter amazement the four sweet little figures came out beautifully!

"Edward got the negative and took it to a specialist in photography who would know a fake at once. Sceptical as he was before he tested it, afterwards he offered £100 down for it. He pronounced it absolutely genuine and a perfectly remarkable photograph. Edward has it enlarged and hanging in his hall. He is very interested in it and as soon as possible he is going to Bradford to see the children. What do you think of this? Edward says the fairies are on the same line of evolution as the *winged* insects, etc. etc. I fear I cannot follow all his reasonings, but I knew you would be keenly interested. I wish you could see that photo and another one of the girls playing with the quaintest goblin imaginable!"

This letter filled me with hopes, and I renewed my pursuit of the photographs. I learned that they were two in number and that they had been sent for inspection to Miss Blomfield, a friend of the family. My chase turned, therefore, in that direction, and in reply to a letter of inquiry I received the following answer:

THE MYRTLES, BECKENHAM,
June 21, 1920.

DEAR SIR,

I am sending the two fairy pictures; they *are* interesting, are they not?

I am sure my cousin would be pleased for you to see them. But he said (and wrote it to me afterwards) that he did not want them to be used in any way at present. I believe he has plans in regard to them, and the pictures are being copyrighted. I don't think the copyright will be his. He has not yet finished his investigations. I asked him if I might photograph them myself so as to have a few prints to give to friends interested, but he wrote that he would rather nothing was done at present.

I think my cousin is away from home just now. But his name is Edward L. Gardner, and he is President of one of the branches of the Theosophical Society (Blavatsky Lodge), and he lectures fairly often at their Hall (Mortimer Hall, Mortimer Square, W.). He lectured there a few weeks ago, and showed the fairies on the screen and told what he knew about them.

Yours sincerely,

E. BLOMFIELD.

This letter enclosed the two very remarkable photographs which are reproduced in this volume, that which depicted the dancing goblin, and the other of wood elves in a ring. An explanatory note setting forth the main points of each is appended to the reproductions. I was naturally delighted at the wonderful pictures, and wrote back thanking Miss Blomfield for her courtesy, and suggesting that an inquiry should be set on foot which would satisfy me as to the genuine nature of the photographs. If this were clearly established I hoped that I might be privileged to help Mr. Gardner in giving publicity to the discovery. In reply I had the following letter:

THE MYRTLES, BECKENHAM,
June 23, 1920.

DEAR SIR ARTHUR,

I am so glad you like the fairies! I should be only too glad to help in any way if I could, but there is so little I can do. Had the photographs been mine (I mean the negatives), I should have been most pleased that anything so lovely in the way of information should have been introduced to the public under such auspices. But it would, as things are, be necessary to ask my cousin. I believe he *wants* people to know, but, as I wrote before, I do not know his plans, and I'm not sure if he is ready.

It has occurred to me since writing to you that it would have been better had I given you his sister's address. She is a most sensible and practical person, much engaged in social work, with which her sympathetic nature and general efficiency make her very successful.

She believes the fairy photographs to be quite genuine. Edward is a clever man—and a good one. His evidence on any of the affairs of life would, I am sure, be considered most reliable by all who knew him, both for veracity and sound judgment. I hope these details will not bore you, but I thought perhaps some knowledge of the people who, so to say, "discovered" the photographs would help in taking you *one* step nearer the source. I do not see any opening for fraud or hoax, though at first when I saw the prints I thought there must be some other explanation than the simple one that they were what they seemed. They appeared too good to be true! But every little detail I have since heard has added to my conviction that they are genuine; though I have only what Edward tells me to go upon. He is hoping to obtain more from the same girls.

Yours sincerely,
E. BLOMFIELD.

At about the same time I received a letter from another lady who had some knowledge of the matter. It ran thus:

29 CROFTDOWN ROAD, HIGHGATE ROAD, N.W.,
June 24, 1920.

DEAR SIR ARTHUR,

I am glad to hear that you are interested in the fairies. If they were really taken, as there seems good reason to believe, the event is no less than the discovery of a new world. It may not be out of place to mention that when I examined them with a magnifying glass I noticed, as an artist, that the hands do not appear to be quite the same as ours. Though the little figures look otherwise so human, the hands seemed to me something like this. (There followed a sketch of a sort of fin.) The beard in the little gnome seems to me to be some sort of insect-like appendage, though it would, no doubt, be called a beard by a clairvoyant seeing him. Also it occurs to me that the whiteness of the fairies may be due to their lack of shadow, which may also explain their somewhat artificial-looking flatness.

Yours sincerely,
MAY BOWLEY.

I was now in a stronger position, since I had actually seen the photographs and learned that Mr. Gardner was a solid person with a reputation for sanity and character. I therefore wrote to him stating the links by which I had reached him, and saying how interested I was in the whole matter, and how essential it seemed that the facts should be given to the public, so that free investigation might be possible before it was too late. To this letter I had the following reply:

5 CRAVEN ROAD, HARLESDEN, N.W.10.
June 25, 1920.

DEAR SIR,

Your interesting letter of the 22nd has just reached me, and very willingly I will assist you in any way that may be possible.

With regard to the photographs, the story is rather a long one and I have only gathered it by going very carefully. The children who were concerned are very shy and reserved indeed . . . . They are of a mechanic's family of Yorkshire, and the children are said to have played with fairies and elves in the woods near their village since babyhood. I will not attempt to narrate the story here, however—perhaps we may meet for that—but when I at length obtained a view of the rather poor prints it so impressed me I begged for the actual negatives. These I submitted to two first-class photographic experts, one in London and one in Leeds. The first, who was unfamiliar with such matters, declared the plates to be perfectly genuine and unfaked, but inexplicable! The second, who did know something of the subject and had been instrumental in exposing several "psychic" fakes, was also entirely satisfied. Hence I proceeded.

I am hopeful of getting more photographs, but the immediate difficulty is to arrange for the two girls to be together. They are 16 or 17 years old and beginning to work and are separated by a few miles. It may be we can manage it and thus secure photographs of the other varieties besides those obtained. These nature spirits are of the non-individualized order and I should greatly like to secure some of the higher. But two children such as these are, are rare, and I fear now that we are late because almost certainly the inevitable will shortly happen, one of them will "fall in love" and then—hey presto!!

By the way, I am anxious to avoid the money consideration. I may not succeed, but would far rather not introduce it. We are out for Truth, and nothing soils the way so quickly. So far as I am concerned you shall have everything I can properly give you.

Sincerely yours,

(SGD.) EDW. L. GARDNER.

This letter led to my going to London and seeing Mr. Gardner, whom I found to be quiet, well-balanced, and reserved—not in the least of a wild or visionary type. He showed me beautiful enlargements of these two wonderful pictures, he gave me much information which is embodied in my subsequent account. Neither he nor I had actually seen the girls, and it was arranged that he should handle the personal side of the matter, while I should examine the results and throw them into literary shape. It was arranged between us that he should visit the village as soon as convenient, and make the acquaintance of everyone concerned. In the meantime, I showed the positives, and sometimes the negatives, to several friends whose opinion upon psychic matters I respected.

Of these Sir Oliver Lodge holds a premier place. I can still see his astonished and interested face as he gazed at the pictures, which I placed before him in the hall of the Athenæum Club. With his usual caution he refused to accept them at their face value, and suggested the theory that the Californian Classical dancers had been taken and their picture superimposed upon a rural British background. I argued that we had certainly traced the pictures to

two children of the artisan class, and that such photographic tricks
would be entirely beyond them, but I failed to convince him, nor
am I sure that even now he is whole-hearted in the matter.

My most earnest critics came from among the spiritualists, to
whom a new order of being as remote from spirits as they are from
human beings was an unfamiliar idea, and who feared, not
unnaturally, that their intrusion would complicate that spiritual
controversy which is vital to so many of us. One of these was a
gentleman whom I will call Mr. Lancaster, who, by a not unusual
paradox, combined considerable psychic powers, including both
clairvoyance and clairaudience, with great proficiency in the
practice of his very prosaic profession. He had claimed that he had
frequently seen these little people with his own eyes, and I,
therefore, attached importance to his opinion. This gentleman had
a spirit guide (I have no objection to the smile of the sceptic), and
to him he referred the question. The answer showed both the
strength and the weakness of such psychic inquiries. Writing to me
in July 1920, he said:

"*Re Photographs*: The more I think of it the less I like it (I mean
the one with the Parisian-coiffed fairies). My own guide says it was
taken by a fair man, short, with his hair brushed back; he has a
studio with a lot of cameras, some of which are 'turned by a
handle.' He did not make it to sell Spiritualists a 'pup,' but did it to
please the little girl in the picture who wrote fairy stories which he
illustrated in this fashion. He is not a Spiritualist, but would laugh
very much if anyone was taken in by it. He does not live near
where we were, and the place is all different, i.e the houses, instead
of being in straight lines, are dropped about all over the place.
Apparently he was not English. I should think it was either
Denmark or Los Angeles by the description, which I give you for
what it is worth.

"I should very much like the lens which would take persons in
rapid motion with the clarity of the photo in question, it must
work at F/4.5 and cost fifty guineas if a penny, and not the sort of
lens one would imagine the children in an artisan's household

would possess in a hand camera. And yet with the speed with which it was taken the waterfall in the background is blurred sufficiently to justify a one second's exposure at least. What a doubting Thomas! I was told the other day that, in the unlikely event of my ever reaching heaven, I should (*a*) Insist on starting a card file index of the angels, and (*b*) Starting a rifle range to guard against the possibility of invasion from Hell. This being my unfortunate reputation at the hands of the people who claim to know me must discount my criticisms as carping—to a certain extent, at all events."

These psychic impressions and messages are often as from one who sees in a glass darkly and contain a curious mixture of truth and error. Upon my submitting this message to Mr. Gardner he was able to assure me that the description was, on the whole, a very accurate one of Mr. Snelling and his surroundings, the gentleman who had actually handled the negatives, subjected them to various tests and made enlarged positives. It was, therefore, this intermediate incident, and not the original inception of the affair, which had impressed itself upon Mr. Lancaster's guide. All this is, of course, quite non-evidential to the ordinary reader, but I am laying all the documents upon the table.

Mr. Lancaster's opinion had so much weight with us, and we were so impressed by the necessity of sparing no possible pains to get at truth, that we submitted the plates to fresh examination, as detailed in the following letter:

5 Craven Road, Harlesden, N.W.10,
July 12, 1920.

Dear Sir Arthur,

Just a line to report progress and acknowledge your kind letters and enclosure from Kodak's.

A week back, after your reference to Mr. Lancaster's opinion, I thought I would get a more careful examination of the negatives made than before, though that was searching enough. So I went over to Mr. Snelling's at Harrow and had a long interview with him, again impressing him with the importance of being utterly certain. I told you, I think, that this Mr. Snelling has had a varied and expert connection of over thirty years with the Autotype Company and Illingworth's large photographic factory and has himself turned out some beautiful work in natural and artificial studio studies. He recently started for himself at Wealdstone (Harrow) and is doing well.

Mr. Snelling's report on the two negatives is positive and most decisive. He says he is perfectly certain of two things connected with these photos, namely:

1. One exposure only;
2. All the figures of the fairies moved during exposure, which was "instantaneous."

As I put all sorts of pressing questions to him, relating to paper or cardboard figures, and backgrounds and paintings, and all the artifices of the modern studio, he proceeded to demonstrate by showing me other negatives and prints that certainly supported his view. He added that anyone of considerable experience could detect the dark background and double exposure in the negative at once. Movement was as easy, as he pointed out in a crowd of aeroplane photos he had by him. I do not pretend to follow all his points, but I am bound to say he thoroughly convinced me of the above two, which seem to me to dispose of all the objections hitherto advanced when they are taken together! Mr S. is willing to make any declaration embodying the above and stakes his reputation unhesitatingly on their truth.

I am away from London from Wednesday next till the 28th when I go on to Bingley for one or two days' investigation on the spot. I propose that you have the two negatives, which are carefully packed and can be posted safely, for this fortnight or so. If you would rather not handle them I will send them to Mr. West of Kodak's, or have them taken to him for his opinion, for I think, as you say, it would be worth having, if he has had direct and extensive practical experience.

I am very anxious now to see this right through, as, though I felt pretty sure before, I am more than ever satisfied now after that interview the other day.

Yours sincerely,
EDW. L. GARDNER.

After receiving this message and getting possession of the negatives I took them myself to the Kodak Company's Offices in Kingsway, where I saw Mr. West and another expert of the Company. They examined the plates carefully, and neither of them could find any evidence of superposition, or other trick. On the other hand, they were of opinion that if they set to work with all their knowledge and resources they could produce such pictures by natural means, and therefore they would not undertake to say that these were preternatural. This, of course, was quite reasonable if the pictures are judged only as technical productions, but it rather savours of the old discredited anti-spiritualistic argument that because a trained conjurer can produce certain effects under his own conditions, therefore some woman or child who gets similar effects must get them by conjuring. It was clear that at the last it was the character and surroundings of the children upon which the inquiry must turn, rather than upon the photos themselves. I had already endeavoured to open up human relations with the elder girl by sending her a book, and I had received the following little note in reply from her father:

31 MAIN STREET, COTTINGLEY, BINGLEY,
July 12, 1920.

DEAR SIR,

I hope you will forgive us for not answering your letter sooner and thanking you for the beautiful book you so kindly sent to Elsie. She is delighted with it. I can assure you we do appreciate the honour you have done her. The book came last Saturday morning an hour after we had left for the seaside for our holidays, so we did not receive it until last night. We received a letter from Mr. Gardner at the same time, and he proposes coming to see us at the end of July. Would it be too long to wait until then, when we could explain what we know about it?

Yours very gratefully,
ARTHUR WRIGHT.

It was evident, however, that we must get into more personal touch, and with this object Mr. Gardner went North and interviewed the whole family, making a thorough investigation of the circumstances at the spot. The result of his journey is given in the article which I published in the *Strand Magazine*, which covers all the ground. I will only add the letter he wrote to me after his return from Yorkshire.

5 CRAVEN ROAD, HARLESDEN, N.W.10,
July 31, 1920.

MY DEAR CONAN DOYLE,

Yours just to hand, and as I have now had an hour to sort things out I write at once so that you have the enclosed before you at the earliest moment. You must be very pressed, so I put the statement as simply as possible, leaving you to use just what you think fit. Prepared negatives, prints of quarter, half-plate, and enlarged sizes, and lantern slides, I have all here.

Also on Tuesday I shall have my own photographs of the valley scenery including the two spots shown in the fairy prints, and also prints of the two children taken in 1917 with their shoes and stockings off, just as they played in the beck at the rear of their house. I also have a print of Elsie showing her hand.

With regard to the points you raise:

1. I have definite leave and permission to act as regards the use made of these photographs in any way I think best.

Publication may be made of them, the only reserve being that full names and addresses shall be withheld.

2. Copies are ready here for England and U.S.A.

3. . . . . The Kodak people and also the Illingworth Co. are unwilling to testify. The former, of course, you know of. Illlingworths claim that they could produce, by means of clever

studio painting and modelling, a similar negative. Another Company's expert made assertions concerning the construction of the "model" that I found were entirely erroneous directly I saw the real ground! They, however, barred any publication. The net result, besides Snelling's views, is that the photograph *could* be produced by studio work, but there is no evidence *positively* of such work in the negatives. (I might add that Snelling, whom I saw again yesterday evening, scouts the claim that such negatives could be produced. He states that he would pick such a one out without hesitation!)

4. My report is enclosed and you are at perfect liberty to use this just as you please.

The father, Mr. Arthur Wright, impressed me favourably. He was perfectly open and free about the whole matter. He explained his position—he simply did not understand the business, but is quite clear and positive that the plate he took out of the Midg camera was the one he put in the same day. His work is that of electrician to an estate in the neighbourhood near. He is clear-headed and very intelligent, and gives one the impression of being open and honest. I learnt the reason of the family's cordial treatment of myself. Mrs. Wright, a few years back, came into touch with theosophical teachings and speaks of these as having done her good. My own connection with the Theosophical Society she knew of and this gave them confidence. Hence the very cordial reception I have met with, which somewhat had puzzled me.

By the way, I think "L's" guide ran up against innocent little Snelling! He matches the description quite well, as I realized last night. And he did prepare the new negatives from which the prints you have were made, and he has a room full up with weird machines with handles and devices used in photography. . . .

Sincerely yours,
EDW. L. GARDNER.

I trust that the reader will agree that up to this point we had not proceeded with any undue rashness or credulity, and that we had taken all common-sense steps to test the case, and had no alternative, if we were unprejudiced seekers for truth, but to go ahead with it, and place our results before the public, so that others might discover the fallacy which we had failed to find. I must apologize if some of the ground in the *Strand* article which follows has already been covered in this introductory chapter.

CHAPTER II

The First Published Account—
Strand Christmas Number, 1920

Should the incidents here narrated, and the photographs attached, hold their own against the criticism which they will excite, it is no exaggeration to say that they will mark an epoch in human thought. I put them and all the evidence before the public for examination and judgment. If I am myself asked whether I consider the case to be absolutely and finally proved, I should answer that in order to remove the last faint shadow of doubt I should wish to see the result repeated before a disinterested witness. At the same time, I recognize the difficulty of such a request, since rare results must be obtained when and how they can. But short of final and absolute proof, I consider, after carefully going into every possible source of error, that a strong *prima-facie* case has been built up. The cry of "fake" is sure to be raised, and will make some impression upon those who have not had the opportunity of knowing the people concerned, or the place. On the photographic side every objection has been considered and adequately met. The pictures stand or fall together. Both are false, or both are true. All the circumstances point to the latter alternative, and yet in a matter involving so tremendous a new departure one needs over-powering evidence before one can say that there is no conceivable loophole for error.

It was about the month of May in this year that I received the information from Miss Felicia Scatcherd, so well known in several departments of human thought, to the effect that two photographs of fairies had been taken in the North of England under circumstances which seemed to put fraud out of the question. The statement would have appealed to me at any time, but I happened at the moment to be collecting material for an article on fairies, now completed, and I had accumulated a surprising number of cases of people who claimed to be able to see these little creatures. The evidence was so complete and detailed, with such good names attached to it, that it was difficult to believe that it was false; but, being by nature of a somewhat sceptical turn, I felt that something closer was needed before I could feel personal conviction and assure myself that these were not thought-forms conjured up by the imagination or expectation of the seers. The rumour of the photographs interested me deeply, therefore, and following the matter up from one lady informant to another, I came at last upon Mr. Edward L. Gardner, who has been ever since my most efficient collaborator, to whom all credit is due. Mr. Gardner, it may be remarked, is a member of the Executive Committee of the Theosophical Society, and a well-known lecturer upon occult subjects.

He had not himself at that time mastered the whole case. but all he had he placed freely at my disposal. I had already seen prints of the photographs, but I was relieved to find that he had the actual negatives, and that it was from them, and not from the prints, that two expert photographers, especially Mr. Snelling of 26 The Bridge, Wealdstone, Harrow, had already formed their conclusions in favour of the genuineness of the pictures. Mr. Gardner tells his own story presently, so I will simply say that at that period he had got into direct and friendly touch with the Carpenter family. We are compelled to use a pseudonym and to withhold the exact address for it is clear that their lives would be much interrupted by correspondence and callers if their identity were too clearly indicated. At the same time there would be, no doubt, no objection to a small committee of inquiry verifying the facts for themselves if this anonymity were respected. For the present, however, we shall simply call them the Carpenter family in the village of Dalesby, West Riding.

Some three years before, according to our information, the daughter and the niece of Mr. Carpenter, the former being sixteen and the other ten years of age, had taken the two photographs—the one in summer, the other in early autumn. The father was quite agnostic in the matter, but as his daughter claimed that she and her cousin when they were together continually saw fairies in the wood and had come to be on familiar and friendly terms with them, he entrusted her with one plate in his camera. The result was the picture of the dancing elves, which considerably amazed the father when he developed the film that evening. The little girl looking across at her playmate, to intimate that the time had come to press the button, is Alice, the niece, while the older girl, who was taken some months later with the quaint gnome, is Iris, the daughter. The story ran that the girls were so excited in the evening that one pressed her way into the small dark-room in which the father was about to develop, and that as she saw the forms of the fairies showing through the solution she cried out to the other girl, who was palpitating outside the door: "Oh, Alice, Alice, the fairies are on the plate—they are on the plate!" It was indeed a triumph for the children, who had been smiled at, as so many children are smiled at by an incredulous world for stating what their own senses have actually recorded.

The father holds a position of trust in connection with some local factory, and the family are well known and respected. That they are cultivated is shown by the fact that Mr. Gardner's advances towards them were made more easy because Mrs. Carpenter was a reader of theosophical teachings and had gained spiritual good from them. A correspondence had arisen and all their letters were frank and honest, professing some amazement at the stir which the affair seemed likely to produce.

Thus the matter stood after my meeting with Mr. Gardner, but it was clear that this was not enough. We must get closer to the facts. The negatives were taken round to Kodak, Ltd., where two experts wee unable to find any flaw, but refused to testify to the genuineness of them, in view of some possible trap. An amateur photographer of experience refused to accept them on the ground

A. FRANCES AND THE FAIRIES.

Photograph taken by Elsie. Bright sunny day in July 1917. The "Midg" camera. Distance 4 ft. Time, 1/50th sec. The original negative is asserted by expert photographers to bear not the slightest trace of combination work, retouching, or anything whatever to mark it is other than a perfectly straight single-exposure photograph, taken in the open air under natural conditions. The negative is sufficiently, indeed somewhat over-exposed. The waterfall and rocks are about 20 ft. behind Frances, who is standing against the bank of the beck. A fifth fairy may be seen between and behind the two on the right. The colouring of the fairies is described by the girls as being of very pale pink green, lavender, and mauve, most marked in the wings and fading to almost pure white in the limbs and drapery. Each fairy has its own special colour.

of the elaborate and Parisian coiffure of the little ladies. Another photographic company, which it would be cruel to name, declared that the background consisted of theatrical properties, and that therefore the picture was a worthless fake. I leaned heavily upon Mr. Snelling's whole-hearted endorsement, quoted later in this article, and also consoled myself by the broad view that if the local conditions were as reported, which we proposed to test, then it was surely impossible that a little village with an amateur photographer could have the plant and the skill to turn out a fake which could not be detected by the best experts in London.

The matter being in this state, Mr. Gardner volunteered to go up at once and report—an expedition which I should have wished to share had it not been for the pressure of work before my approaching departure for Australia. Mr. Gardner's report is here appended:

5 CRAVEN ROAD, HARLESDEN, N.W.10,
July 29, 1920.

It was early in this year, 1920, that I heard from a friend of photographs of fairies having been successfully taken in the North of England. I made some inquiries, and these led to prints being sent to me with the names and address of the children who were said to have taken them. The correspondence that followed seemed so innocent and promising that I begged the loan of the actual negatives—and two quarter-plates came by post a few days after. One was a fairly clear one, the other much under-exposed.

The negatives proved to be truly astonishing photographs indeed, for there was no sign of double exposure nor anything other than ordinary straightforward work. I cycled over to Harrow to consult an expert photographer of thirty years' practical experience whom I knew I could trust for a sound opinion. Without any explanation I passed the plates over and asked what he thought of them. After examining the "fairies" negative carefully, exclamations began: "This is the most extraordinary thing I've ever seen!" "Single exposure!" "Figures have moved!" "Why, it's a genuine photograph! Wherever did it come from?"

I need hardly add that enlargements were made and subjected to searching examination—without any modification of opinion. The immediate upshot was that a "positive" was taken from each negative, that the originals might be preserved carefully untouched, and then new negatives were prepared and intensified to serve as better printing mediums. The originals are just as received and in my keeping now. Some good prints and lantern slides were soon prepared.

In May I used the slides, with others, to illustrate a lecture given in the Mortimer Hall, London, and this aroused considerable interest, largely because of these pictures and their story. A week or so later I received a letter from Sir A. Conan Doyle asking for information concerning them, some report, I understood, having reached him from a mutual friend. A meeting with Sir Arthur followed, and the outcome was that I agreed to hasten my proposed personal investigation into the origin of the photographs, and carry this through at once instead of waiting till September, when I should be in the North on other matters.

In consequence, to-day, July 29, I am just back in London from one of the most interesting and surprising excursions that it has ever been my fortune to make!

We had time, before I went, to obtain opinions on the original negatives from other expert photographers, and one or two of these were adverse rather than favourable. Not that any would say positively that the photographs were faked, but two did claim that they *could* produce the same class of negative by studio work involving painted models, etc., and it was suggested further that the little girl in the first picture was standing behind a table heaped up with fern and moss, that the toad-stool was unnatural, that in the gnome photo the girl's hand was not her own, that uniform shading was questionable, and so on. All of this had its weight, and though I went North with as little bias one way or the other as possible, I felt quite prepared to find that a personal investigation would disclose some evidence of falsity.

The lengthy journey completed, I reached a quaint, old-world village in Yorkshire, found the house, and was cordially received. Mrs. C. and her daughter I. (the girl as shown playing with the gnome) were both at home to meet me, and Mr. C., the father, came in shortly afterwards.

Several of the objections raised by the professionals were disposed of almost at once, as, a half-hour after reaching the house, I was exploring a charming little valley, directly at the rear, with a stream of water running through, where the children had been accustomed to see and play with the fairies. I found the bank behind which the child, with her shoes and stockings off, is shown as standing; toad-stools exactly as in the photograph were about in plenty, quite as big and hearty-looking. And the girl's hand? Well, she laughingly made me promise not to say much about it, it is so very long! I stood on the spots shown and easily identified every feature. Then, in course of eliciting all that one could learn about the affair, I gathered the following, which, for the sake of conciseness, I set out below:

Camera used: "The Midg" quarter-plate. Plates: Imperial Rapid.
Fairies photo: July 1917. Day brilliantly hot and sunny. About 3 p.m. Distance: 4 feet. Time: 1–50th second.
Gnome photo: September 1917. Day bright, but not as above. About 4 o'clock. Distance: 8 feet. Time: 1–50th second.

I. was sixteen years old: her cousin A. was ten years. Other photographs were attempted but proved partial failures, and plates were not kept.

Colouring: The palest of green, pink, mauve. Much more in the wings than in the bodies, which are very pale to white. The gnome is described as seeming to be in black tights, reddish-brown jersey, and red pointed cap. He was swinging his pipes, holding them in his left hand and was just stepping up on to I.'s knee when A. snapped him.

A., the visiting cousin, went away soon after, and I. says they must be together to "take photographs." Fortunately they will meet in a few weeks' time, and they promise me to try to get some more. I. added she would very much like to send me one of a fairy flying.

Mr. C's. testimony was clear and decisive. His daughter had pleaded to be allowed to use the camera. At first he demurred, but ultimately, after dinner one Saturday, he put just one plate in the Midg and gave it to the girls. They returned in less than an hour and begged him to develop the plate as I. had "taken a photograph." He did so, with, to him, the bewildering result shown in the print of the fairies!

Mrs. C. says she remembers quite well that the girls were only away from the house a short time before they brought the camera back.

Extraordinary and amazing as these photographs may appear, I am now quite convinced of their entire genuineness, as indeed would everyone else be who had the same evidence of transparent honesty and simplicity that I had. I am adding nothing by way of explanations or theories of my own, though the need for two people, preferably children, is fairly obvious for photography, in order to assist in the strengthening of the etheric bodies. Beyond this I prefer to leave the above statement as a plain, unvarnished narrative of my connection with the incidents.

I need only add that no attempt appears ever to have been made by the family to make these photographs public, and whatever has been done in that direction locally has not been pressed by any of them, nor has there been any money payment in connection with them.

EDWARD L. GARDNER.

I may add as a footnote to Mr. Gardner's report that the girl informed him in conversation that she had no power of any sort over the actions of the fairies, and that the way to " 'tice them," as she called it, was to sit passively with her mind quietly turned in that direction; then, when faint stirrings or movements in the distance heralded their presence, to beckon towards them and show that they were welcome. It was Iris who pointed out the pipes of the gnome, which we had both taken as being the markings of the moth-like under-wing. She added that if there was not too much rustling in the wood it was possible to hear the very faint and high sound of the pipes. To the objections of photographers that the fairy figures show quite different shadows to those of the human our answer is that ectoplasm, as the etheric protoplasm has been named, has a faint luminosity of its own, which would largely modify shadows.

To the very clear and, as I think, entirely convincing report of Mr. Gardner's, let me add the exact words which Mr. Snelling, the expert photographer, allows us to use. Mr. Snelling has shown great strength of mind, and rendered signal service to psychic study, by taking a strong line, and putting his professional reputation as an expert upon the scales. He has had a varied connection of over thirty years with the Autotype Company and Illingworth's large photographic factory, and has himself turned out some beautiful work of every kind of natural and artificial studio studies. He laughs at the idea that any expert in England could deceive him with a faked photograph. "These two negatives," he says, "are entirely genuine, unfaked photographs of single exposure, open-air work, show movement in the fairy figures, and there is no trace whatever of studio work involving card or paper models, dark backgrounds, painted figures, etc. In my opinion, they are both straight untouched pictures."

A second independent opinion is equally clear as to the genuine character of the photographs, founded upon a large experience of practical photography.

There is our case, fortified by pictures of the places which the unhappy critic has declared to be theatrical properties. How well we know that type of critic in all our psychic work, though it is not always possible to at once show his absurdity to other people.

I will now make a few comments upon the two pictures, which I have studied long and earnestly with a high-power lens.

One fact of interest is this presence of a double pipe—the very sort which the ancients associated with fauns and naiads—in each picture. But if pipes, why not everything else? Does it not suggest a complete range of utensils and instruments for their own life?

B. ELSIE AND THE GNOME

Photograph taken by Frances. Fairly bright day in September 1917. The "Midg" camera. Distance, 8 ft. Time, 1/50th sec. The original negative has been tested, enlarged, and analysed in the same exhaustive manner as A. This plate was badly under-exposed. Elsie was playing with the gnome and beckoning it to come on to her knee. The gnome leapt up just as Frances, who had the camera, snapped the shutter. He is described as wearing black tights, a reddish-brown jersey, and a pointed bright-red cap, The wings are more moth-like than the fairies and of a soft, downy, neutral tint. The music of the pipes held in his left hand can just be heard as a tiny tinkle sometimes if all is still. No weight is perceptible, though when on the bare hand a fairy feels like a "little breath."

Their clothing is substantial enough. It seems to me that with fuller knowledge and with fresh means of vision these people are destined to become just as solid and real as the Eskimos. There is an ornamental rim to the pipe of the elves which shows that the graces of art are not unknown among them. And what joy is in the complete abandon of their little graceful figures as they let themselves go in the dance! They may have their shadows and trials as we have, but at least there is a great gladness manifest in this demonstration of their life.

A second general observation is that the elves are a compound of the human and the butterfly, while the gnome has more of the moth. This may be merely the result of under-exposure of the negative and dullness of the weather. Perhaps the little gnome is really of the same tribe, but represents an elderly male, while the elves are romping young women. Most observers of fairy life have reported, however, that there are separate species, varying very much in size, appearance and locality—the wood fairy, the water fairy, the fairy of the plains, etc.

Can these be thought-forms? The fact that they are so like our conventional idea of fairies is in favour of the idea. But if they move rapidly, have musical instruments, and so forth, then it is impossible to talk of "thought-forms," a term which suggests something vague and intangible. In a sense we are all thought-forms, since we can only be perceived through the senses, but these little figures would seem to have an objective reality, as we have ourselves, even if their vibrations should prove to be such that it takes either psychic power or a sensitive plate to record them. If they are conventional it may be that fairies have really been seen in every generation and so some correct description of them has been retained.

There is one point of Mr. Gardner's investigation which should be mentioned. It had come to our knowledge that Iris could draw, and had actually at one time done some designs for a jeweller. This naturally demanded caution, though the girl's own frank nature is, I understand, a sufficient guarantee for those who know her. Mr. Gardner, however, tested her powers of drawing, and found that, while she could do landscapes cleverly, the fairy figures which she had attempted in imitation of those she had seen were entirely uninspired, and bore no possible resemblance to those in the photograph. Another point which may be commended to the careful critic with a strong lens is that the apparent pencilled face at the side of the figure on the right is really only the edge of her hair, and not, as might appear, a drawn profile.

I must confess that after months of thought I am unable to get the true bearings of this event. One or two consequences are obvious. The experiences of children will be taken more seriously. Cameras will be forthcoming. Other well-authenticated cases will come along. These little folk who appear to be our neighbours, with only some small difference of vibration to separate us, will become familiar. The thought of them, even when unseen, will add a charm to every brook and valley and give romantic interest to every country walk. The recognition of their existence will jolt the material twentieth-century mind out of its heavy ruts in the mud, and will make it admit that there is a glamour and a mystery to life. Having discovered this, the world will not find it so difficult to accept that spiritual message supported by physical facts which has already been so convincingly put before it. All this I see, but there may be much more. When Columbus knelt in prayer upon the edge of America, what prophetic eye saw all that a new continent might do to affect the destinies of the world? We also seem to be on the edge of a new continent, separated not by oceans but by subtle and surmountable psychic conditions. I look at the prospect with awe. May those little creatures suffer from the contact and some Las Casas bewail their ruin! If so, it would be an evil day when the world defined their existence. But there is a guiding hand in the affairs of man, and we can but trust and follow.

CHAPTER III

Reception of the First Photographs

Though I was out of England at the time, I was able, even in Australia, to realise that the appearance of the first photographs in the *Strand Magazine* had caused very great interest. The press comments were as a rule cautious but not unsympathetic. The old cry of "Fake!" was less conspicuous than I had expected, but for some years the press has been slowly widening its views upon psychic matters, and is not so inclined as of old to attribute every new manifestation to fraud. Some of the Yorkshire papers had made elaborate inquiries, and I am told that photographers for a considerable radius from the house were cross-questioned to find if they were accomplices. *Truth*, which is obsessed by the idea that the whole spiritualistic movement all everything connected with it is one huge, senseless conspiracy to deceive, concocted by knaves and accepted by fools, had the usual contemptuous and contemptible articles, which ended by a prayer to Elsie that she should finish her fun and let the public know how it really was done. The best of the critical attacks was in the *Westminster Gazette*, who sent a special commissioner to unravel the mystery, and published the result on January 12, 1921. By kind permission I reproduce the article:

Left: Elsie and Frances. A snapshot taken by Mr Wright in June 1917, with the 'Midg' camera he had just obtained – his first and only camera.
Below: Cottingley Beck and Glen are marked A, B, C, D, E, and the cottage with an X.

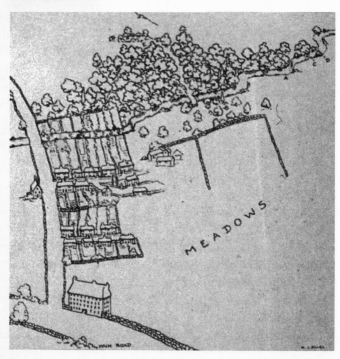

DO FAIRIES EXIST?

INVESTIGATION IN A YORKSHIRE VALLEY
COTTINGLEY'S MYSTERY

STORY OF THE GIRL WHO TOOK THE SNAPSHOT

The publication of photographs of fairies—or, to be more explicit, one photograph of fairies and another of a gnome—playing round children has aroused considerable interest, not only in Yorkshire, where the beings are said to exist, but throughout the country.

The story, mysterious as it was when first told, became even more enigmatical by reason of the fact that Sir A. Conan Doyle made use of fictitious names in his narrative in the *Strand Magazine* in order, as he says, to prevent the lives of the people concerned being interrupted by callers and correspondence. That he has failed to do. I am afraid Sir Conan does not know Yorkshire people, particularly those of the dales, because any attempt to hide identity immediately arouses their suspicions, if it does not go so far as to condemn the writer for his lack of frankness.

It is not surprising, therefore, that his story is accepted with reserve. Each person to whom I spoke of the subject during my brief sojourn in Yorkshire dismissed the matter curtly as being untrue. It has been the principal topic of conversation for weeks, mainly because identity had been discovered.

My mission to Yorkshire was to secure evidence, if possible, which would prove or disprove the claim that fairies existed. I frankly confess that I failed.

The particular fairyland is a picturesque little spot off the beaten track, two or three miles from Bingley. Here is a small village called Cottingley, almost hidden in a break in the upland, through which tumbles a tiny stream, known as Cottingley Beck, on its way to the Aire, less than a mile away. The "heroine" of Sir Conan Doyle's story is Miss Elsie Wright[1], who resides with her parents at 31

[1] From this time onwards the real name Wright is used instead of Carpenter as in the original article—the family having withdrawn their objection.

Lynwood Terrace. The little stream runs past the back of the house, and the photographs were taken not more than a hundred yards away. When Miss Wright made the acquaintance of the fairies she was accompanied by her cousin, Frances Griffiths, who resides at Dean Road, Scarborough.

One photograph, taken by Miss Wright in the summer of 1917, when she was sixteen, shows her cousin, then a child of ten, with a group of four fairies dancing in the air before her, and in the other, taken some months afterwards, Elsie, seated on the grass, has a quaint gnome dancing beside her.

There are certain facts which stand out clearly and which none of the evidence I was able to obtain could shake. No other people have seen the fairies, though everybody in the little village knew of their alleged existence; when Elsie took the photograph she was unacquainted with the use of a camera, and succeeded at the first attempt; the girls did not invite a third person to see the wonderful visitors, and no attempt was made to make the discovery public.

First I interviewed Mrs. Wright, who, without hesitation, narrated the whole of the circumstances without adding any comment. The girls, she said, would spend the whole of the day in the narrow valley, even taking their lunch with them, though they were within a stone's throw of the house. Elsie was not robust, and did not work during the summer months, so that she could derive as much benefit as possible from playing in the open. She had often talked about seeing the fairies, but her parents considered it was nothing more than childish fancy, and let it pass. Mr. Wright came into possession of a small camera in 1917, and one Saturday afternoon yielded to the persistent entreaties of his daughter and allowed her to take it out. He placed one plate in position, and explained to her how to take a "snap." The children went away in high glee and returned in less than an hour, requesting Mr. Wright to develop the plate. While this was being done Elsie noticed that the fairies were beginning to show, and exclaimed in an excited tone to her cousin, "Oh, Frances, the fairies are on the plate!" The second photograph was equally successful, and a few prints from each plate were given to friends as curiosities about a year ago. They evidently attracted little notice until one was shown to some of the delegates at a Theosophical Congress in Harrogate last summer.

Mrs. Wright certainly gave me the impression that she had no desire to keep anything back, and answered my questions quite frankly. She told me that Elsie had always been a truthful girl, and there were neighbours who accepted the story of the fairies simply on the strength of their knowledge of her. I asked about Elsie's career, and her mother said that after she left school she worked a few months for a photographer in Manningham Lane, Bradford, but did not care for running errands most of the day. The only other work she did there was "spotting." Neither occupation was likely to teach a fourteen-year-old girl how to "fake" a plate. From there she went to a jeweller's shop, but her stay there was not prolonged. For many months immediately prior to taking the first photograph she was at home and did not associate with anyone who possessed a camera.

At that time her father knew little of photography, "only what he had picked up by dodging about with the camera," as he put it, and any suggestion that he had faked the plate must be dismissed.

When he came home from the neighbouring mill, and was told the nature of my errand, he said he was "fed up" with the whole business, and had nothing else to tell. However, he detailed the story I had already heard from his wife, agreeing in every particular, and Elsie's account, given to me in Bradford, added nothing. Thus I had the information from the three members of the family at different times, and without variation. The parents confessed they had some difficulty in accepting the photographs as genuine and even questioned the girls as to how they faked them. The children persisted in their story, and denied any act of dishonesty. Then they "let it go at that." Even now their belief in the existence of the fairies is merely an acceptance of the statements of their daughter and her cousin.

I ascertained that Elsie was described by her late schoolmaster as being "dreamy," and her mother said that anything imaginative appealed to her. As to whether she could have drawn the fairies when she was sixteen I am doubtful. Lately she has taken up water-

Elsie in 1920, standing near where the Gnome was taken in 1917.

Frances in 1920.

colour drawing, and her work, which I carefully examined, does not reveal that ability in a marked degree, though she possesses a remarkable knowledge of colour for an untrained artist.

Sir A. Conan Doyle says that at first he was not convinced that the fairies were not thought-forms conjured up by the imagination or expectation of the seers. Mr. E. L. Gardner, a member of the Executive Committee of the Theosophical Society, who made an investigation on the spot and also interviewed all the members of the family, records his opinion that the photographs are genuine.

Later in the day I went to Bradford, and at Sharpe's Christmas Card Manufactory saw Miss Wright. She was working in an upper room, and at first refused to see me, sending a message to the effect that she did not desire to be interviewed. A second request was successful, and she appeared at a small counter at the entrance to the works.

She is a tall, slim girl, with a wealth of auburn hair, through which a narrow gold band, circling her head, was entwined.

Like her parents, she just said she had nothing to say about the photographs, and, singularly enough, used the same expression as her father and mother —"I am 'fed up' with the thing."

She gradually became communicative, and told me how she came to take the first photograph.

Asked where the fairies came from, she replied that she did not know.

"Did you see them come?" I asked; and on receiving an affirmative reply, suggested that she must have noticed where they came from.

Miss Wright hesitated, and laughingly answered, "I can't say." She was equally at a loss to explain where they went after dancing near her, and was embarrassed when I pressed for a fuller explanation. Two or three questions went unanswered, and my suggestion that they must have "simply vanished into the air" drew the monosyllabic reply, "Yes." They did not speak to her, she said, nor did she speak to them.

When she had been with her cousin she had often seen them before. They were only kiddies when they first saw them, she remarked, and did not tell anybody.

"But," I went on, "it is natural to expect that a child, seeing fairies for the first time, would tell its mother." Her answer was to repeat that she did not tell anybody. The first occasion on which fairies were seen, it transpired, was in 1915.

In reply to further questions, Miss Wright said she had seen them since, and had photographed them, and the plates were in the possession of Mr. Gardner. Even after several prints of the first lot of fairies had been given to friends, she did not inform anybody that she had seen them again. The fact that nobody else in the village had seen them gave her no surprise. She firmly believed that she and her cousin were the only persons who had been so fortunate, and was actually convinced that nobody else would be.

"If anybody else were there," she said, "the fairies would not come out."

Further questions put with the object of eliciting a reason for that statement were only answered with smiles and a final significant remark "You don't understand."

Miss Wright still believes in the existence of the fairies, and is looking forward to seeing them in the coming summer.

The fairies of Cottingley, as they appeared to the two girls, are fine-weather elves, as Miss Wright said they appeared only when it was bright and sunny; never when the weather was dull or wet.

The strangest part of the girl's story was her statement that in their more recent appearances the fairies were more "transparent" than in 1916 and 1917, when they were "rather hard." Then she added the qualification, "You see, we were young then." This she did not amplify, though pressed to do so.

The hitherto obscure village promises to be the scene of many pilgrimages during the coming summer. There is an old saying in Yorkshire: "Ah'll believe what Ah see," which is still maintained as a valuable maxim.

The general tone of this article makes it clear that the Commissioner would very naturally have been well pleased to effect a *coup* by showing up the whole concern. He was, however, a fair-minded and intelligent man, and has easily exchanged the rôle of Counsel for the Prosecution to that of a tolerant judge. It will be observed that he brought out no new fact which had not already appeared in my article, save the interesting point that this was absolutely the first photograph which the children had ever taken in their lives. Is it conceivable that under such circumstances they could have produced a picture which was fraudulent and yet defied the examination of so many experts? Granting the honesty of the father, which no one has ever impugned, Elsie could only have done it by cut-out images, which must have been of exquisite beauty, of many different models, fashioned and kept without the knowledge of her parents, and capable of giving the impression of motion when carefully examined by an expert. Surely this is a large order!

In the *Westminster* article it is clear that the writer has not had much aquaintance with psychic research. His surprise that a young girl should not know whence appearances come or whither they go, when they are psychic forms materializing in her own peculiar aura, does not seem reasonable. It is a familiar fact also that psychic phenomena are always more active in warm sunny weather than in damp or cold. Finally, the girl's remark that the shapes were getting more diaphanous was a very suggestive one, for it is with childhood that certain forms of mediumship are associated, and there is always the tendency that, as the child becomes the woman, and as the mind becomes more sophisticated and commonplace, the phase will pass. The refining process can be observed in the second series of pictures, especially in the little figure which is holding out the flower. We fear that it has now completed itself, and that we shall have no more demonstrations of fairy life from this particular source.

One line of attack upon the genuine character the photographs was the production of a fake, and the argument: "There, you see how good that is, and yet it is an admitted fake. How can you be sure that yours are not so also?" The fallacy of this reasoning lay in the fact that these imitations were done by skilled performers, while the originals were by untrained children. It is a repetition of the stale and rotten argument by which the world has been befooled so long, that because a conjurer under his own conditions can imitate certain effects, therefore the effects themselves ever existed.

It must be admitted that some of these attempts were very well done, though none of them passed the scrutiny of Mr. Gardner or myself. The best of them was by a lady photographer connected with the Bradford Institute, Miss Ina Inman, whose production was so good that it caused us for some weeks to regard it with an open mind. There was also a weird but effective arrangement by Judge Docker, of Australia. In the case of Miss Imnan's elves, clever as they were, there nothing of the natural grace and freedom of movement which characterize the wonderful Cottingley fairy group.

Among the more remarkable comments in the press was one from Mr. George A. Wade in the London *Evening News* of December 8, 1920. It told of a curious sequence of events in Yorkshire, and ran as follows:

"Are there real fairies in the land to-day? The question has been raised by Sir Arthur Conan Doyle, and there have been submitted photographs which purport to be those of actual 'little people.'

"Experiences which have come within my own knowledge may help to throw a little light on this question as to whether there are real fairies, actual elves and gnomes, yet to be met with in the dales of Yorkshire, where the photographs are asserted to have been taken.

"Whilst spending a day last year with my friend, Mr. Halliwell Sutcliffe, the well-known novelist, who lives in that district, he told me, to my intense surprise, that he personally knew a schoolmaster not far from his home who had again and again insisted that he had seen, talked with, and had played with real fairies in some meadows not far away! The novelist mentioned this to me as an actual curious fact, for which he, himself, had no explanation. But he said that the man was one whose education, personality, and character made him worthy of credence—a man not likely to harbour a delusion or to wish to deceive others.

"Whilst in the same district I was informed by a man whom I knew to be thoroughly reliable that a young lady living in Skipton had mentioned to him more than once that she often went up to— (a spot in the dales the name of which he gave) to 'play and dance with the fairies!' When he expressed astonishment at the statement she repeated it, and averred that it was really true!

"In chatting about the matter with my friend, Mr. William Riley, the author of *Windyridge*, *Netherleigh*, and *Jerry and Ben*, a writer who knows the Yorkshire moors and dales intimately, Mr. Riley asserted that though he had never seen actual fairies there, yet he knew several trustworthy moorland people whose belief in them was unshakable and who persisted against all contradiction that they themselves had many times seen pixies at certain favoured spots in Upper Airedale and Wharfedale.

"When some time later an article of mine anent these things was published in a Yorkshire newspaper, there came a letter from a lady at a distance who stated that the account confirmed a strange experience which she had when on holiday in the same dale up above Skipton.

"She stated that one evening, when walking alone on the higher portion of a slope of the hills to her intense astonishment she saw in a meadow close below her fairies and sprites playing and dancing in large numbers. She imagined that she must be dreaming, or under some hallucination, so she pinched herself and rubbed her eyes to make sure that she was really awake. Convinced of this, she looked again, and still unmistakably saw the 'little people.' She gave a full account of how they played, of the long time she watched them, and how at length they vanished. Without a doubt she was convinced of the truth of her statement.

"What can we make of it all? My own mind is open, but it is difficult to believe that so many persons, unknown to one another, should have conspired to state what is false. It is a remarkable coincidence, if nothing more, that the girls in Sir Arthur Conan Doyle's account, the schoolmaster mentioned by Mr. Sutcliffe, the young woman who came from Skipton, and the lady who wrote to the Yorkshire newspaper should all put the spot where the fairies are to be seen almost within a mile or two of one another.

"Are there real fairies to be met with there?"

The most severe attack upon the fairy pictures seems to have been that of Major Hall-Edwards, the famous authority upon radium, in the *Birmingham Weekly Post*. He said:

"Sir Arthur Conan Doyle takes it for granted that these photographs are real photographs of fairies, notwithstanding the fact that no evidence has so far been put forward to show exactly how they were produced. Anyone who has studied the extraordinary effects which have from time to time been obtained by cinema operators must be aware that it is possible, given time and opportunity, to produce by means of faked photographs almost anything that can be imagined.

"It is well to point out that the elder of the two girls has been described by her mother as a most imaginative child, who has been in the habit of drawing fairies for years, and who for a time was apprenticed to a firm of photographers. In addition to this she has access to some of the most beautiful dales and valleys, where the imagination of a young person is easily quickened.

"One of the pictures represents the younger child leaning on her elbow upon a bank, while a number of fairies are shown dancing around her. The child does not look at the fairies, but is posing for the photograph in the ordinary way. The reason given for her apparent disinterestedness in the frolicsome elves is that she is used to the fairies, and was merely interested in the camera.

"The picture in question could be 'faked' in two ways. Either the little figures of the fairies were stuck upon a cardboard, cut out and placed close to the sitter, when, of course, she would not be able to see them, and the whole photograph produced on a marked plate; or the original photograph, without 'fairies,' may have had stuck on it the figures of fairies cut from some publication. This would then be rephotographed and, if well done, no photographer could swear that the second negative was not the original one.

"Major Hall-Edwards went on to remark that great weight had

been placed upon the fact that the fairies in the photograph had transparent wings, but that a tricky photographer could very easily reproduce such an effect.

" 'It is quite possible,' he observed, 'to cut off the transparent wings of insects and paste them on a picture of fairies. It is easy to add the transparent wings of large flies and so arrange them that portions of the photograph can be viewed through the wings and thus obtain a very realistic effect.'

"It has been pointed out that although the 'fairies' are represented as if they were dancing—in fact they are definitely stated to be dancing—there is no evidence of movement in the photographs. An explanation of this has been given by the photographer herself, who has told us that the movements of the fairies are exceedingly slow and might be compared to the retarded-movement films shown in the cinemas. This proves that the young lady possesses a very considerable knowledge of photography.

"Millions of photographs have been taken by operators of different ages—children and grown-ups—of country scenes and places which, we have been taught, are the habitats of nymphs and elves; yet until the arrival upon the scene of these two wonderful children the image of a fairy has never been produced on a photographic plate. On the evidence I have no hesitation in saying that these photographs could have been 'faked.' I criticize the attitude of those who declared there is something supernatural in the circumstances attending the taking of these pictures because, as a medical man, I believe that the inculcation of such absurd ideas into the minds of children will result in later life in manifestations of nervous disorder and mental disturbances. Surely young children can be brought up to appreciate the beauties of Nature without their imagination being filled with exaggerated, if picturesque, nonsense and misplaced sentiment."

To this Mr. Gardner answered:

"Major Hall-Edwards says 'no evidence has been put forward to show how they were produced.' The least a would-be critic should do is surely to read the report of the case. Sir A. Conan Doyle is asserted to have taken it 'for granted that these photographs are real and genuine.' It would be difficult to misrepresent the case more completely. The negatives and contact prints were submitted to the most searching tests known to photographic science by experts, many of whom were frankly sceptical. They emerged as being unquestionably single-exposure plates and, further, as bearing no evidence whatever in themselves of any trace of the innumerable faking devices known. This did not clear them entirely, for, as I have always remarked in my description of the investigation, it is held possible by employing highly artistic and skilled processes to produce similar negatives. Personally, I should very much like to see this attempted seriously. The few that have been done, though very much better than the crude examples Major Hall-Edwards submits, break down hopelessly on simple analysis.

"The case resolved itself at an early stage into the examination of the personal element and the motive for faked work. It was this that occupied us so strenuously, for we fully realized the imperative need of overwhelmingly satisfying proof of personal integrity before accepting the photographs as genuine. This was carried through, and its thoroughness may be estimated by the fact that, notwithstanding the searching nature of the investigation that has followed the publication of the village, names, etc., nothing even modifies my first report. I need hardly point out that the strength of the case lies in its amazing simplicity and the integrity of the family concerned. It is on the photographic plus the personal evidence that the case stands.

"Into part of the criticism advanced by Major Hall-Edwards it will be kinder, perhaps, not to enter. Seriously to suggest that a visit to a cinema show and the use of an apt illustration implies 'a very considerable knowledge of photography' is on a par with the supposition that to be employed as an errand girl and help in a shop indicates a high degree of skill in that profession! We are not quite so credulous as that, nor were we able to believe that two children, alone and unaided, could produce in half an hour a faked photograph of the type of 'Alice and the Fairies.' "

In addition to this criticism by Major Hall-Edwards there came an attack in *John o' London* from the distinguished writer Mr. Maurice Hewlett, who raises some objections which were answered in Mr. Gardner's subsequent reply. Mr. Hewlett's contention was as follows:

"The stage which Sir A. Conan Doyle has reached at present is one of belief in the genuineness of what one may call the Carpenter photographs, which showed the other day to the readers of the *Strand Magazine* two ordinary girls in familiar intercourse with winged beings, as near as I can judge, about eighteen inches high. If he believes in the photographs two inferences can be made, so to speak, to stand up: one, that he must believe also in the existence of the beings; two, that a mechanical operation, where human agency has done nothing but prepare a plate, focus an object, press a button, and print a picture, has rendered visible something which is not otherwise visible to the common naked eye. That is really all Sir Arthur has to tell us. He believes the photographs to be genuine. The rest follows. But why does he believe it? Because the young ladies tell him that they are genuine. Alas!

"Sir Arthur cannot, he tells us, go into Yorkshire himself to cross-examine the young ladies, even if he wishes to cross-examine them, which does not appear. However, he sends in his place a friend, Mr. E. L. Gardner, also of hospitable mind, with settled opinions upon theosophy and kindred subjects, but deficient, it would seem, in logical faculty. Mr. Gardner has himself photographed in the place where the young ladies photographed each other, or thereabouts. No winged beings circled about him, and one wonders why Mr. Gardner (*a*) was photographed, (*b*) reproduced the photograph in the *Strand Magazine*.

"The only answer I can find is suggested to me by the appearance of the Virgin and Child to certain shepherds in a peach-orchard at Verona. The shepherds told their parish priest that the Virgin Mary had indeed appeared to them on a moonlit night, had accepted of a bowl of milk from them, had then picked a peach from one of the trees and eaten it. The priest visited the spot in their company, and in due course picked up a peach-stone. That settled it. Obviously the Madonna had been really there, for here was the peach-stone to prove it.

"I am driven to the conclusion that Mr. Gardner had himself photographed on a particular spot in order to prove the genuineness of former photographs taken there. The argument would run: The photographs were taken on a certain spot; but I have been myself photographed on that spot; therefore the photographs were genuine. There is a fallacy lurking, but it is a hospitable fallacy; and luckily it doesn't very much matter.

"The line to take about a question of the sort is undoubtedly that of least resistance. Which is the harder of belief, the faking of a photograph or the objective existence of winged beings eighteen inches high? Undoubtedly, to a plain man, the latter; but assume the former. If such beings exist, if they are occasionally visible, and if a camera is capable of revealing to all the world what is hidden from most people in it, we are not yet able to say that the Carpenter photographs are photographs of such beings. For we, observe, have not seen such beings. True: but we have all seen photographs of beings in rapid motion—horses racing, greyhounds coursing a hare, men running over a field, and so on. We have seen pictures of these things, and we have seen photographs of them; and the odd thing is that never, never by any chance does the photograph of a running object in the least resemble a picture of it.

The horse, dog, or man, in fact, in the photograph does not look to be in motion at all. And rightly so, because in the instant of being photographed *it was not in motion*. So infinitely rapid is the action of light on the plate that it is possible to isolate a fraction of time in a rapid flight and to record it. Directly you combine a series of photographs in sequence, and set them moving, you have a semblance of motion exactly like that which you have in a picture.

"Now, the beings circling round a girl's head and shoulders in the Carpenter photograph are in *picture flight*, and not in photographic flight. That is certain. They are in the approved pictorial, or plastic, convention of dancing. They are not well

Elsie seated on the bank where the
fairies were dancing in 1917 (photo
1920).

The fall of water just above the site of
the last photograph.

rendered by any means. They are stiff compared with, let us say, the whirling gnomes on the outside wrapper of *Punch*. They have very little of the wild, irresponsible vagary of a butterfly. But they are an attempt to render an aerial dance—pretty enough in a small way. The photographs are too small to enable me to decide whether they are painted on cardboard or modelled in the round; *but the figures are not moving.*

"One other point, which may be called a small one—but in a matter of the sort no point is a small one. I regard it as a certainty, as the other plainly is. If the dancing figures had been dancing beings, really there, the child in the photograph would have been looking at them, not at the camera. I know children.

"And knowing children, and knowing that Sir Arthur Conan Doyle has legs, I decide that the Miss Carpenters have pulled one of them. Meantime I suggest to him that epochs are born, not made."

To which Mr. Gardner replied in the following issue:

"I could have wished that Mr. Maurice Hewlett's somewhat playful criticism of the genuineness of the photographs of fairies appearing in the *Strand Magazine* Christmas number had been more clearly defined. The only serious point raised is the difference between photographic and pictorial representation of motion— Mr. Hewlett maintaining that the latter is in evidence in the photographs.

"With regard to the separate photographs of the sites, surely the reason for their inclusion is obvious. Photographic experts had stated that though the two negatives revealed no trace of any faking process (such as double exposure, painted figures on enlargements rephotographed, set-up models in card or other material), still it could not be held to be impossible to obtain the same class of result by very clever studio work. Also, certain points that needed elucidation were the haze above and at the side of the child's head, and the blurred appearance of the waterfall as compared with the clarity of the figures, etc. An inspection of the spots and photographs of their surroundings was surely the only way to clear up some of these. As a matter of fact, the waterfall proved to be about twenty feet behind the child, and hence out of focus, and some large rocks at the same distance in the rear, at the side of the fall, were found to be the cause of the haziness. The separate photographs, of which only one is published of each place, confirm entirely the genuineness of the sites—not the genuineness of the fairies.

"In commenting on the photography of a moving object, Mr. Hewlett makes the astonishing statement that at the instant of being photographed *it is not in motion* (Mr. H.'s italics). I wonder when it is, and what would happen if a camera was exposed then! Of course the moving object is in motion during exposure, no matter whether the time be a fiftieth or a millionth part of a second, though Mr. Hewlett is by no means the only one to fall into this error. And each of the fairy figures in the negative discloses signs of movement. This was one of the first points determined.

"I admit at once, of course, that this does not meet the criticism that the fairies display much more grace in action than is to be found in the ordinary snapshot of a moving horse or man. But if we are here dealing with fairies whose bodies must be presumed to be of a purely ethereal and plastic nature, and not with skeleton-framed mammals at all, is it such a very illogical mind that accepts the exquisite grace therein found as a natural quality that is never absent? In view of the overwhelming evidence of genuineness now in hand this seems to be the truth.

"With regard to the last query raised—the child looking at the camera instead of at the fairies—Alice was entirely unsophisticated respecting the proper photographic attitude. For her, cameras were much more novel than fairies and never before had she seen one used so close to her. Strange to us as it may seem, at the moment it interested her the most. Apropos, would a faker, clever enough to produce such a photograph, commit the elementary blunder of not posing his subject?"

Among other interesting and weighty opinions, which were in

general agreement with our contentions, was one by Mr. H. A. Staddon of Goodmayes, a gentleman who had made a particular hobby of fakes in photography. His report is too long and too technical for inclusion, but, under the various headings of composition, dress, development, density, lighting, poise, texture, plate, atmosphere, focus, halation, he goes very completely into the evidence, coming to the final conclusion that when tried by all these tests the chances are not less than 80 per cent. in favour of authenticity.

It may be added that in the course of exhibiting these photographs (in the interests of the Theosophical bodies with which Mr. Gardner is connected), it has sometimes occurred that the plates have been enormously magnified upon the screen. In one instance, at Wakefield, the powerful lantern used threw an exceptionally large picture on a huge sheet. The operator, a very intelligent man who had taken a sceptical attitude, was entirely converted to the truth of the photographs, for, as he pointed out, such an enlargement would show the least trace of a scissors irregularity or of any artificial detail, and would make it absurd to suppose that a dummy figure could remain undetected. The lines were always beautifully fine and unbroken.

CHAPTER IV

—————

The Second Series

When Mr. Gardner was in Yorkshire in July, he left a good camera with Elsie, for he learned that her cousin Frances was about to visit her again and that there would be a chance of more photographs. One of our difficulties has been that the associated aura of the two girls is needful. This joining of auras to produce a stronger effect than either can get singly is common enough in psychic matters. We wished to make full use of the combined power of the girls in August. My last words to Mr. Gardner, therefore, before starting for Australia were that I should open no letter more eagerly than that which would tell me the result of our new venture. In my heart I hardly expected success, for three years had passed, and I was well aware that the processes of puberty are often fatal to psychic power.

I was surprised, therefore, as well as delighted, when I had his letter at Melbourne, informing of complete success and enclosing three more wonderful prints, all taken in the fairy glen. Any doubts which had remained in my mind as to honesty were completely overcome, for it was clear that these pictures, specially the one of the fairies in the bush, were altogether beyond the possibility of fake. Even now, however, having a wide experience of transference of pictures in psychic photography and the effect of thought upon ectoplasmic images, I feel that there is a possible alternative explanation in this direction, and I have never quite lost sight of the fact that it is a curious coincidence that so unique an event should have happened in a family some members of which were already inclined to occult study, and might be imagined to have formed thought-pictures of occult appearances. Such suppositions, though not to be entirely dismissed, are, as it seems to me, far-fetched and remote.

Here is the joyous letter which reached me at Melbourne:

September 6, 1920.

MY DEAR DOYLE,

Greetings and best wishes! Your last words to me before we parted were that you would open my letter with the greatest interest. You will not be disappointed—for the wonderful thing has happened!

I have received from Elsie three more negatives taken a few days back. I need not describe them, for enclosed are the three prints in a separate envelope. The "Flying Fairy" and the "Fairies' Bower" are the most amazing that any modern eye has ever seen surely! I received these plates on Friday morning last and have since been thinking furiously.

A nice little letter came with them saying how sorry they were (!) that they couldn't send more, but the weather had been bad (it has been abominably cold), and on only two afternoons had Elsie and Frances been able to visit the glen. (Frances has now returned to Scarborough at the call of school.) All quite simple and straightforward and concluding with the hope that I might be able to spend another day with them at the end of this month.

I went over to Harrow at once, and Snelling without hesitation pronounced the three as bearing the same proofs of genuineness as the fist two, declaring further that at any rate the 'bower" one was utterly beyond any possibility of faking! While on this point I might add that to-day I have interviewed Illingworth's people and somewhat to my surprise they enclosed this view. (Now if you have not yet opened the envelope please do so and I will continue . . .)

I am going to Yorkshire on the 23rd inst. to fill some lecture engagements and shall spend a day at C., and of course take photos

C. FRANCES AND THE LEAPING FAIRY.

Photograph taken by Elsie in August 1920. "Cameo" camera. Distance, 3 ft. Time, 1/50th sec. This negative and the two following (D and E) have been as strictly examined as the earlier ones, and similarly disclose no trace of being other than perfectly genuine photographs. Also they proved to have been taken from the packet given them, each plate having been privately marked unknown to the girls. The fairy is leaping up from the leaves below and hovering for a moment — it had done so three or four times. Rising a little higher than before, Frances thought it would touch her face and involuntarily tossed her head back. The fairy is apparently in a close-fitting costume of faint lavender colour.

of these spots and examine and take away any "spoilt" negatives that will serve as useful accompaniments. The bower negative, by the way, the girls simply could not understand at all. They saw the sedate-looking fairy to the right, and without waiting to get in the picture Elsie pushed the camera close up to the tall grasses and took the snap. . . .

To this letter I made answer as follows:

MELBOURNE,
October 21, 1920.

DEAR GARDNER,

My heart was gladdened when out here in far Australia I had your note and the three wonderful prints which are confirmatory of our published results. You and I needed no confirmation, but the whole line of thought will be so novel to the ordinary busy man who has not followed psychic inquiry, that he will need that it be repeated again and yet again before he realizes that this new order of life is really established and has to be taken into serious account, just as the pigmies of Central Africa.

I felt guilty when I laid a delay-action mine and left the country, leaving you to face the consequences of the explosion. You knew, however, that it was unavoidable. I rejoice now that you should have this complete shield against those attacks which will very likely take the form of a clamour for further pictures, unaware that such pictures actually exist.

The matter does not bear directly upon the more vital question of our own fate and that of those we have lost, which has brought me out here. But anything which extends man's mental horizon, and proves to him that matter as we have known it is not really the limit of our universe, must have a good effect in breaking down materialism and leading human thought to a broader and more spiritual level.

It almost seems to me that those wise entities who are conducting this campaign from the other side, and using some of us as humble instruments have recoiled before that sullen stupidity against which Goethe said the Gods themselves fight in vain, and have opened up an entirely new line of advance, which will turn that so-called "religious," and essentially irreligious, position, which has helped to bar our way. They can't destroy fairies by antediluvian texts, and when once fairies are admitted other psychic phenomena will find a more ready acceptance.

Goodbye, my dear Gardner, I am proud to have been associated with you in this epoch-making incident. We have had continued messages at seances for some time that a visible sign was coming through—and perhaps this was what is meant. The human race does not deserve fresh evidence, since it has not troubled, as a rule, to examine that which already exists. However, our friends beyond are very long-suffering and more charitable than I, for I will confess that my soul is filled with a cold contempt for the muddle-headed indifference and the moral cowardice which I see around me.

Yours sincerely,
ARTHUR CONAN DOYLE.

The next letters from Mr. Gardner told me that in September, immediately after this second series was taken, he had gone north again, and came away more convinced than ever of the honesty of the whole Wright family and of the genuine nature of the photographs. From this letter I take the following extracts:

"My visit to Yorkshire was very profitable. I spent the whole day with the family and took photographs of the new sites, which proved to be in close proximity to the others. I enclose a few prints of these. It was beside the pond shown that the 'cradle' or bower photograph was taken. The fairy that is in the air was leaping rather than flying. It had leapt up from the bush below five or six times, Elsie said, and seemed to hover at the top of its spring. It was about the fifth time that it did so that she snapped the shutter. Unfortunately, Frances thought the fairy was leaping on to her face, the action was so vigorous, and tossed her head back. The motion can be detected in the print. The fairy who is looking at

Elsie in the other photograph is holding a bunch of fairy hare-bells. I thought this one had 'bobbed' hair and was altogether quite in the fashion, her dress is so up-to-date! But Elsie says her hair was close-curled, not bobbed. With regard to the 'cradle' Elsie tells me they both saw the fairy on the right and the demure-looking sprite on the left, but not the bower. Or rather, she says there was only a wreath of faint mist in between and she could make nothing of it. We have now succeeded in bringing this print out splendidly, and as I can get certificates from experts giving the opinion that this negative could not possibly be 'faked' we seem to be on perfectly safe ground. The exposure times in each case were one-fiftieth of a second, the distance about three to four feet, the camera was the selected 'Cameo' that I had sent to Elsie, and the plates were of those that I had sent too.

"The colours of dresses and wings, etc., I have complete, but will post these particulars on when writing at length a little later and have the above more fully written out." . . .

November 27, 1920.
"The photographs:

"When I was in Yorkshire in September investigating the second series, I took photos of the spots, of course, and the full account of the success. The children only had two brief hours or so of decent sunshine during the whole of that fortnight they were together in August. On the Thursday they took two and on the Saturday one. If it had been normal weather we might have obtained a score or more. Possibly, however, it is better to go slowly—though I propose we take the matter further again in May or June. The camera I had sent was the one used, and also the plates (which had all been marked privately by the Illingworth Co., independently of me). The three new fairy negatives proved to be of these and can be certified so to be by the manager. The Cradle or Bower negative is, as I think I told you, declared to be utterly unfakeable, and I can get statements to this effect. . . ."

In a subsequent fuller account Mr. Gardner says:

D. FAIRY OFFERING POSY OF HARE-BELLS TO ELSIE.
The fairy is standing still, poised on the bush leaves. The wings
are shot with yellow, and upper part of dress is very pale pink.

"On Thursday afternoon August 26, a fairly bright and sunny day, fortunately (for the unseasonably cold weather experienced generally could hardly have been worse for the task), a number of photographs were taken, and again on Saturday, August 28. The three reproduced here are the most striking and amazing of the number. I only wish every reader could see the superlatively beautiful enlargements made directly from the actual negatives. The exquisite grace of the flying fairy baffles description—all fairies, indeed, seem to be super-Pavlovas in miniature. The next, of the fairy offering a flower—an etheric hare-bell—to Iris, is a model of gentle and dignified pose, but it is to the third that I would draw special and detailed attention. Never before, or otherwise, surely, has a fairy's bower been photographed!

"The central ethereal cocoon shape, something between a cocoon and an open chrysalis in appearance, lightly suspended amid the grasses, is the bower or cradle. Seated on the upper left-hand edge with wing well displayed is an undraped fairy apparently considering whether it is time to get up. An earlier riser of more mature age is seen on the right possessing abundant hair and wonderful wings. Her slightly denser body can be glimpsed within her fairy dress. Just beyond, still on the right, is the clear-cut head of a mischievous but smiling elf wearing a close-fitting cap. On the extreme left is a demure-looking sprite, with a pair of very diaphanous wings, while just above, rather badly out of focus, however, is another with wings and widely extended, and with outspread arms, apparently just alighting on the grass tops. The face in half profile can just be traced in a very clear and carefully toned print that I have. Altogether, perhaps, this of the bower is the most astonishing and interesting of the more successful photographs, though some may prefer the marvellous grace of the flying figure.

"The comparative lack of definition in this photograph is probably accounted for by the absence of the much denser human element. To introduce us in this way directly to a charming bower of the fairies was quite an unexpected result on the part of the girls, by the way. They saw the somewhat sedate fairy on the right in the long grasses, and, making no attempt this time to get in the picture

E. FAIRIES AND THEIR SUN-BATH

This is especially remarkable, as not only would it be exceedingly difficult to produce such a negative by faked work—impossible in the opinion of some experts—but it contains a feature that was quite unknown to the girls. The sheath or cocoon appearing in the midst of the grasses had never been seen by them before, and they had no idea what it was. Fairy lovers and observers, of the New Forest and elsewhere, describe it as a magnetic bath, woven very quickly by the fairies, and used after dull weather and in the autumn especially. The sun's rays through the sheath appear to magnetise the interior, and thus provide a "bath" that restores vitality and vigour.

themselves, Iris put the camera very close up and obtained the snap. It was simply good fortune that the bower was close by. In showing me the negative, Iris only remarked it as being a quaint little picture that she could not make out!"

There the matter stands, and nothing has occurred from that time onwards to shake the validity of the photographs. We were naturally desirous of obtaining more, and in August 1921 the girls were brought together once again, and the very best photographic equipment, including a stereoscopic camera and a cinema camera, were placed at their disposal. The Fates, however, were most unkind, and a combination of circumstances stood in the way of success. There was only a fortnight during which Frances could be at Cottingley, and it was a fortnight of almost incessant rain, the long drought breaking at the end of July in Yorkshire. In addition, a small seam of coal had been found in the Fairy Glen, and it had been greatly polluted by human magnetism. These conditions might perhaps have been overcome, but the chief impediment of all was the change in the girls, the one through womanhood and the other through board-school education.

There was one development, however, which is worth recording. Although they were unable to materialize the images to such an extent as to catch them upon a plate, the girls had not lost their clairvoyant powers, and were able, as of old, to see the spirits and elves which still abounded in the glen. The sceptic will naturally say that we have only their own word for that, but this is not so. Mr. Gardner had a friend, whom I will call Mr. Sergeant, who held a commission in the Tank Corps in the war, and is an honourable gentleman with neither the will to deceive nor any conceivable object in doing so. This gentleman has long had the enviable gift of clairvoyance in a very high degree, and it occurred to Mr. Gardner that we might use him as a check upon the statements of the girls. With great good humour, he sacrificed a week of his scanty holiday—for he is a hard-worked man—in this curious manner. But the results seem to have amply repaid him. I have before me his reports, which are in the form of notes made as he actually watched the phenomena recorded. The weather was, as stated, bad on the whole, though clearing occasionally. Seated with the girls, he saw all that they saw, and more, for his powers proved to be considerably greater. Having distinguished a psychic object, he would point in the direction and ask them for a description, which he always obtained correctly within the limit of their powers. The whole glen, according to his account, was swarming with many forms of elemental life, and he saw not only wood-elves, gnomes, and goblins, but the rarer undines, floating over the stream. I take a long extract from his rather disjointed notes, which may form a separate chapter.

──────────

CHAPTER V

Observations of a Clairvoyant in the Cottingley Glen, August 1921

Gnomes and Fairies. In the field we saw figures about the size of the gnome. They were making weird faces and grotesque contortions at the group. One in particular took great delight in knocking his knees together. These forms appeared to Elsie singly—one dissolving and another appearing in its place. I, however, saw them in a group with one figure more prominently visible than the rest. Elsie saw also a gnome like the one in the photograph, but not so bright and not coloured. I saw a group of female figures playing a game, somewhat resembling the children's game of oranges and lemons. They played in a ring; the game resembled the grand chain in the Lancers. One fairy stood in the centre of the ring more or less motionless, while the remainder, who appeared to be decked with flowers and to show colours, not normally their own, danced round her. Some joined hands and made an archway for the others, who moved in and out as in a maze. I noticed that the result of the game appeared to be the forming of a vortex of force which streamed upwards to an apparent distance of four or five feet above the ground. I also noticed that in those parts of the field where the grass was thicker and darker, there appeared to be a correspondingly extra activity among the fairy creatures.

Water Nymph. In the beck itself, near the large rock, at a slight fall in the water, I saw a water sprite. It was an entirely nude female figure with long fair hair, which it appeared to be combing or passing through its fingers. I was not sure whether it had any feet or not. Its form was of a dazzling rosy whiteness, and its face very beautiful. The arms, which were long and graceful, were moved with a wave-like motion. It sometimes appeared to be singing, though no sound was heard. It was in a kind of cave, formed by a projecting piece of rock and some moss. Apparently it had no wings, and it moved with a sinuous, almost snake-like motion, in a semi-horizontal position. Its atmosphere and feeling was quite different from that of the fairies. It showed no consciousness of my presence, and, though I waited with the camera the hope of taking it, it did not detach itself from the surroundings in which it was in some way merged.

Wood Elves. (Under the old beeches in the wood, Cottingley, August 12, 1921.) Two tiny wood elves came racing over the ground past us as we sat on a fallen tree trunk. Seeing us, they pulled up short about five feet away, and stood regarding us with considerable amusement but no fear. They appeared as if completely covered in a tight-fitting one-piece skin, which shone slightly as if wet. They had hands and feet large and out of proportion to their bodies. Their legs were somewhat thin, ears large and pointed upwards, being almost pear-shaped. There were a large number of these figures racing about the ground. Their noses appeared almost pointed and their mouths wide. No teeth and no structure inside the mouth, not even a tongue, so far as I could see. It was as if the whole were made up of a piece of jelly. Surrounding them, as an etheric double surrounds a physical form, is a greenish light, something like chemical vapour. As Frances came up and sat within a foot of them they withdrew, as if in alarm, a distance of eight feet or so, where they remained apparently regarding us and comparing notes of their impressions. These two live in the roots of a huge beech tree—they disappeared through a crevice into which they walked (as one might walk into a cave) and sank below the ground.

Water Fairy. (August 14, 1921.) By a small waterfall, which threw up a fine spray, was seen poised in the spray a diminutive fairy form

A view of the beck in 1921.

of an exceedingly tenuous nature. It appeared to have two main colourings, the upper part of its body and aura being pale violet, the lower portion pale pink. This colouring appeared to penetrate right through aura and denser body, the outline of the latter merging into the former. This creature hung poised, its body curved gracefully backwards, its left arm held high above its head, as if upheld by the vital force in the spray, much as a seagull supports itself against the wind. It was as if lying on its back in a curved position against the flow of the stream. It was human in shape, but I did not show any characteristics of sex. It remained motionless in this position for some moments, then flashed out of view. I did not I notice any wings.

Fairy, Elves, Gnomes, and Brownie. (Sunday, August 14, 9 p.m. In the field.) Lovely still moonlight evening. The field appears to be densely populated with nature spirits of various kinds—a brownie, fairies, elves, and gnomes.

A Brownie. He is rather taller than the normal, say eight inches, dressed entirely in brown with facings of a darker shade, bag-shaped cap, almost conical, knee breeches, stockings, thin ankles, and large pointed feet—like gnomes' feet. He stands facing us, in no way afraid, perfectly friendly and much interested; he gazes wide-eyed upon us with a curious expression as of dawning intellect. It is as if he were reaching after something just beyond his mental grasp. He looks behind him at a group of fairies who are approaching us and moves to one side as if to make way. His mental attitude is semi-dreamlike, as of a child who would say "I can stand and watch this all day without being tired." He clearly sees much of our auras and is strongly affected by our emanations.

Fairies. Frances sees tiny fairies dancing in a circle, the figures gradually expanding in size till they reached eighteen inches, the ring widening in proportion. Elsie sees a vertical circle of dancing fairies flying slowly round; as each one touched the grass he appeared to perform a few quick steps and then continued his slow motion round the circle. The fairies who are dancing have long skirts, through which their limbs be seen; viewed astrally the circle is bathed in golden yellow light, with the outer edges of many

hues, violet predominating. The movement of the fairies is
reminiscent of that of the great wheel at Earl's Court. The fairies
float very slowly, remaining motionless as far as bodies and limbs
are concerned, until they come round to the ground again. There
is a tinkling music accompanying all this. It appears to have more of
the aspect of a ceremony than a game. Frances sees two fairy figures
performing as if on the stage, one with wings, one without. Their
bodies shine with the effect of rippling water in the sun. The fairy
without wings has bent over backwards like a contortionist till its
head touches the ground, while the winged figure bends over it.
Frances sees a small Punch-like figure, with a kind of Welsh hat,
doing a kind of dancing by striking its heel on the ground and at
the same time raising his hat and bowing. Elsie sees a flower fairy,
like a carnation in shape, the head appearing where the stalk
touches the flower and the green sepals forming a tunic from
which the arms protrude, while the petals form a skirt, below
which are rather thin legs. It is tripping across the grass. Its
colouring is pink like a carnation in a pale, suffused sort of way.
(Written by the light the moon.) I see couples a foot high, female
and male, dancing in a slow waltz-like motion in the middle of the
field. They appear even to reverse. They are clothed in etheric
matter and rather ghost-like in appearance. Their bodies are
outlined with grey light and show little detail.

Elsie sees a small imp reminiscent of a monkey, revolving slowly
round a stalk to the top of which he was clinging. He has an impish
face and is looking our way as if performing for our benefit.

The brownie appears during all this to have taken upon himself
the duties of showman. I see what may be described as a fairy
fountain about twenty feet ahead. It is caused by an uprush of fairy
force from the ground—and spreading fishtail fashion higher into
the air—it is many-hued. This was also seen by Frances.

(Monday, August 15. In the field.) I saw three figures racing from
the field into the wood—the same figures previously seen in the
wood. When about a distance of ten yards from the wall they leapt
over it into the wood and disappeared. Elsie sees in centre of field a
very beautiful fairy figure, somewhat resembling a figure of

Mercury, without winged sandals, but has fairy wings. Nude, light curly hair, kneeling down in a dark clump of grass, with its attention fixed on something in the ground. It changes its position; first it is sitting back on its heels, and then it is racing to its full kneeling height. Much larger than usual, probably eighteen inches high. It waves its arms over some object on the ground. It has picked up something from the ground (as I think a baby) and holds it to its breast and seems to be praying. Has Greek features and resembles a Greek statue—like a figure out of a Greek tragedy.

(Tuesday, August 16, 10 p.m. In the field.) By the light of a small photographic lamp.

Fairies. Elsie sees a circle of fairies tripping round, hands joined, facing outwards. A figure appears in the centre of the ring, at the same time the fairies faced inwards.

Goblins. A group of goblins came running towards us from the wood to within fifteen feet of us. They differ somewhat from the wood elves, having more the look of gnomes, though they are smaller, being about the size of small brownies.

Fairy. Elsie sees a beautiful fairy quite near; it is nude, with golden hair, and is kneeling in the grass, looking this way with hands on knees, smiling at us. It has a very beautiful face, and is concentrating its gaze on me. This figure came within five feet of us, and, after being described, faded away.

Elf. Elsie sees a kind of elf who seems to be going so fast that it blows his hair back; one can sense the wind round him, yet he is stationary, though he looks to be busily hurrying along.

Goblins. Elsie sees a flight of little mannikins, imp-like in appearance, descending slantwise on to the grass. They form into two lines which cross each other as they come down. One line is coming vertically down, feet touching head, the other comes across them shoulder to shoulder. On reaching the ground they all run off in different directions, all serious, as if intent upon some business. The elves from the wood appear to be chiefly engaged in racing across the field, though no other purpose appears to be served by their speed or presence. Few of them pass near us without pulling up to stare. The elves seem to be the most curious

The two girls near the spot where the Leaping Fairy was taken in 1920

of all the fairy creatures. Frances sees three and calls them goblins.

Fairy. A blue fairy. A fairy with wings and general colouring of sea-blue and pale pink. The wings are webbed and marked in varying colours like those of a butterfly. The form is perfectly modelled and practically nude. A golden star shines in the hair. This fairy is a director, though not apparently with any band for the present.

Fairy Band. There has suddenly arrived in the field a fairy director with a band of fairy people. Their arrival causes a bright radiance to shine in the field, visible to us sixty yards away. She is very autocratic and definite in her orders, holding unquestioned command. They spread themselves out into a gradually widening circle around her, and as they do so, a soft glow spreads out over the grass. They are actually vivifying and stimulating the growth in the field. This is a moving band which arrives in this field swinging high over the tree tops as if from a considerable distance. Inside a space of two minutes the circle has spread to approximately twelve feet wide and is wonderfully radiant with light. Each member of the band is connected to the leader by a thin stream of light. These streams are of different colour, though chiefly yellow, deepening to orange. They meet in the centre, merging in her aura, and there is a constant flow backwards and forwards among them. The form produced by this is something like an inverted fruit dish, with the central fairy as the stem, and the lines of light which flow in a graceful even curve forming the sides of the bowl. This party is in intense activity, as if it had much to do and little time in which to do it. The director is vivified and instructed from within herself, and appears to have her consciousness seated upon a more subtle plane than that upon which she is working.

Fairy. Elsie sees a tall and stately fairy come across the field to a clump of harebells. It is carrying in its arms something which may be a baby fairy, wrapped in gauzy substance. It lays this in the clump of harebells and kneels down as though stroking something, and after a time fades away. We catch impressions of four-footed creatures being ridden by winged figures who are thin and bend over their mounts like jockeys. It is no known animal which they bestride, having a face something like that of a caterpillar.

Amongst this fairy activity which appears all over the field, one glimpses an occasional gnome-like form walking with serious mien across the field, whilst the wood elves and other imp-like forms run about amongst their more seriously employed fairy kind. All three of us keep seeing weird creatures as of elemental essence.

Elsie sees about a dozen fairies moving towards us in a crescent-shaped flight. As they drew near she remarked with ecstasy upon their perfect beauty of form—even while she did so they became as ugly as sin, as if to give the lie to her words. They all leered at her and disappeared. In this episode it may be that one contacts a phase of the antagonism and dislike which so many of the fairy creatures feel for humans at this stage of evolution.

Frances saw seven wee fairies quite near—weird little figures—lying face downwards.

(In the Glen, 18th, 2 p.m.) Frances sees a fairy as big as herself, clothed in tights and a garment scalloped round the hips; the whole is tight-fitting and flesh-coloured; she has very large wings which she opens above her head; then she raises her arms from her side up above her head and waves them gracefully in the air. She has a very beautiful face with an expression as if inviting Frances into Fairyland. Her hair is apparently bobbed and her wings are transparent.

Golden Fairy. One specially beautiful one has a body clothed in iridescent shimmering golden light. She has tall wings, each of which is almost divided into upper and lower portions. The lower portion, which is smaller than the upper, appears to be elongated to a point like the wings of certain butterflies. She, too, is moving her arms and fluttering her wings. I can only describe her as a golden wonder. She smiles and clearly sees us. She places her finger on her lips. She remains watching us with smiling countenance in amongst the leaves and branches of the willow. She is not objectively visible on the physical plane. She points with her right hand, moving it in a circle round her feet, and I see a number, perhaps six or seven, cherubs (winged faces); these appear to be held in shape by some invisible will. She has cast a fairy spell over me completely subjugating the mental principle—leaves me staring wild-eyed in amongst the leaves and flowers.

An elf-like creature runs up the slanting branchs of the willow from the ground where the fairy stands. He is not a very pleasant visitor—I should describe him as distinctly low class.

CHAPTER VI

Independent Evidence for Fairies

By a curious coincidence, if it be indeed a coincidence, at the moment when the evidence for the actual existence of fairies was brought to my notice, I had just finished an article dealing with the subject, in which I gave particulars of a number of cases where such creatures were said to have been seen, and showed how very strong were the reasons for supposing that some such forms of life exist. I now reproduce this article, and I add to it another chapter containing fresh evidence which reached me after the publication of the photographs in the *Strand Magazine*.

We are accustomed to the idea of amphibious creatures who may dwell unseen and unknown in the depths of the waters, and then some day be spied sunning themselves upon a sandbank, whence they slip into the unseen once more. If such appearances were rare, and if it should so happen that some saw them more clearly than others, then a very pretty controversy would arise, for the sceptics would say, with every show of reason, "Our experience is that only land creatures live on the land, and we utterly refuse to believe in things which slip in and out of the water; if you will demonstrate them to us we will begin to consider the question." Faced by so reasonable an opposition, the others could only mutter that they had seen them with their own eyes, but that they could not command their movements. The sceptics would hold the field.

Something of the sort may exist in our psychic arrangements. One can well imagine that there is a dividing line, like the water edge, this line depending upon what we vaguely call a higher rate of vibrations. Taking the vibration theory as a working hypothesis, one could conceive that by raising or lowering the rate the creatures could move from one side to the other of this line of material visibility, as the tortoise moves from the water to the land, returning for refuge to invisibility as the reptile scuttles back to the surf. This, of course, is supposition, but intelligent supposition based on the available evidence is the pioneer of science, and it may be that the actual solution will be found in this direction. I am alluding now, not to spirit return, where seventy years of close observation has given us some sort of certain and definite laws, but rather to those fairy and phantom phenomena which have been endorsed by so many ages, and still even in these material days seem to break into some lives in the most unexpected fashion.

Victorian science would have left the world hard and clean and bare, like a landscape in the moon; but this science is in truth but a little light in the darkness, and outside that limited circle of definite knowledge we see the loom and shadow of gigantic and fantastic possibilities around us, throwing themselves continually across our consciousness in such ways that it is difficult to ignore them.

There is much curious evidence of varying value concerning these borderland forms, which come or go either in fact or imagination—the latter most frequently, no doubt. And yet there remains a residue which, by all human standards, should point to occasional fact. Lest I should be too diffuse, I limit myself in this essay to the fairies, and, passing all the age-long tradition, which is so universal and consistent, come down to some modern instances which make one feel that this world is very much more complex than we had imagined, and that there may be upon its surface some very strange neighbours who will open up inconceivable lines of science for our posterity, especially if it should be made easier for them, by sympathy or other help, to emerge from the deep and manifest upon the margin.

Taking a large number of cases which lie before me, there are two points which are common to nearly all of them. One is that children claim to see these creatures far more frequently than adults. This may possibly come from greater sensitiveness of apprehension, or it may depend upon these little entities having less fear of molestation from the children. The other is, that more cases are recorded in which they have been seen in the still, shimmering hours of a very hot day than at any other time. "The action of the sun upon the brain," says the sceptic. Possibly—and also possibly not. If it were a question of raising the slower vibrations of our surroundings one could imagine that still, silent heat would be the very condition which might favour such a change. What is the mirage of the desert? What is that scene of hills and lakes which a whole caravan can see while it faces in a direction where for a thousand miles of desert there is neither hill nor lake, nor any cloud or moisture to produce refraction? I can ask the question, but I do not venture to give an answer. It is clearly a phenomenon which is not to be confused with the erect or often inverted image which is seen in a land of clouds and of moisture.

If the confidence of children can be gained and they are led to speak freely, it is surprising how many claim to have seen fairies. My younger family consists of two little boys and one small girl, very truthful children, each of whom tells with detail the exact circumstances and appearance of the creature. To each it happened only once, and in each case it was a single little figure, twice in the garden, once in the nursery. Inquiry among friends shows that many children have had the same experience, but they close up at once when met by ridicule and incredulity. Sometimes the shapes are unlike those which they would have gathered from picture-books. "Fairies are like nuts and moss," says one child in Lady Glenconner's charming study of family life. My own children differ in the height of the creature, which may well vary, but in their dress they are certainly not unlike the conventional idea, which, after all, may also be the true one.

There are many people who have a recollection of these experiences of their youth, and try afterwards to explain them away on material grounds which do not seem adequate or reasonable.

Thus in his excellent book on folk-lore the Rev. S. Baring-Gould gives us a personal experience which illustrates several of the points already mentioned. "In the year 1838," he says, "when I was a small boy of four years old, we were driving to Montpelier on a hot summer day over the long straight road that traverses a pebble- and rubble-strewn plain, on which grows nothing save a few aromatic herbs. I was sitting on the box with my father when, to my great surprise, I saw legions of dwarfs of about two feet high running along beside the horses; some sat laughing on the pole, some were scrambling up the harness to get on the backs of the horses. I remarked to my father what I saw, when he abruptly stopped the carriage and put me inside beside my mother, where, the conveyance being closed, I was out of the sun. The effect was that, little by little, the host of imps diminished in number till they disappeared altogether."

Here, certainly, the advocates of sunstroke have a strong, though by no means a final, case. Mr. Baring-Gould's next illustration is a sounder one.

"When my wife was a girl of fifteen," he says, "she was walking down a lane in Yorkshire, between green hedges, when she saw seated in one of the privet hedges a little green man, perfectly well made, who looked at her with his beady black eyes. He was about a foot or fifteen inches high. She was so frightened that she ran home. She remembers that it was a summer day."

A girl of fifteen is old enough to be a good witness, and her flight and the clear detail of her memory point to a real experience. Again we have the suggestion of a hot day.

Baring-Gould has yet a third case. "One day a son of mine," he says, "was sent into the garden to pick pea-pods for the cook to shell for dinner. Presently he rushed into the house as white as chalk to say that while he was thus engaged, and standing between the rows of peas, he saw a little man wearing a red cap, a green jacket, and brown knee-breeches, whose face was old and wan, and who had a grey beard and eyes as black and hard as sloes. He stared so intently at the boy that the latter took to his heels."

Here, again, the pea-pods show that it was summer, and

probably in the heat of the day. Once again the detail is very exact and corresponds closely, as I shall presently show, to some independent accounts. Mr. Baring-Gould is inclined to put all these down to the heat conjuring up the familiar pictures of fairy books, but some further evidence may cause the reader to doubt this explanation.

Let us compare with these stories the very direct evidence of Mrs. Violet Tweedale, whose courage in making public the result of her own remarkable psychic faculties should meet with recognition from every student of the subject. Our descendants will hardly realize the difficulty which now exists of getting first-hand evidence with names attached, for they will have outgrown the state when the cry of "fake" and "fraud" and "dupe" is raised at once against any observer, however honourable and moderate, by people who know little or nothing of the subject. Mrs. Tweedale says:

"I had a wonderful little experience some five years ago which proved to me the existence of fairies. One summer afternoon I was walking alone along the avenue of Lupton House, Devonshire. It was an absolutely still day—not a leaf moving, and all Nature seemed to sleep in the hot sunshine. A few yards in front of me my eye was attracted by the violent movements of a single long blade-like leaf of a wild iris. This leaf was swinging and bending energetically, while the rest of the plant was motionless. Expecting to see a field-mouse astride it, I stepped very softly up to it. What was my delight to see a tiny green man. He was about five inches long, and was swinging back-downwards. His tiny green feet, which appeared to be green-booted, were crossed over the leaf, and his hands, raised behind his head, also held the blade. I had a vision of a merry little face and something red in the form of a cap on the head. For a full minute he remained in view, swinging on the leaf. Then he vanished. Since then I have several times seen a single leaf moving violently while the rest of the plant remained motionless, but I have never again been able to see the cause of the movement."

Here the dress of the fairy, green jacket and red cap, is exactly the same as was described independently by Baring-Gould's son, and again we have the elements of heat and stillness. It may be fairly answered that many artists have drawn the fairies in such a dress, and that the colours may in this way have been impressed upon the minds of both observers. In the bending iris we have something objective, however, which cannot easily be explained away as a cerebral hallucination, and the whole incident seems to me an impressive piece of evidence.

A lady with whom I have corresponded, Mrs. H., who is engaged in organizing work of the most responsible kind, has had an experience which resembles that of Mrs. Tweedale. "My only sight of a fairy," she says, "was in a large wood in West Sussex, about nine years ago. He was a little creature about half a foot high, dressed in leaves. The remarkable thing about his face was that no soul looked through his eyes. He was playing about in long grass and flowers in an open space." Once again summer is indicated. The length and colour of the creature correspond with Mrs. Tweedale's account, while the lack of soul in the eyes may be compared with the 'hard" eyes described by young Baring-Gould.

One of the most gifted clairvoyants in England was the late Mr. Turvey, of Bournemouth, whose book, *The Beginnings of Seership*, should be in the library of every student. Mr. Lonsdale, of Bournemouth, is also a well-known sensitive. The latter has given me the following account of an incident which he observed some years ago in the presence of Mr. Turvey.

"I was sitting," says Mr. Lonsdale, "in his company in his garden at Branksome Park. We sat in a hut which had an open front looking on to the lawn. We had been perfectly quiet for some time, neither talking nor moving, as was often our habit. Suddenly I was conscious of a movement on the edge of the lawn, which on that side went up to a grove of pine trees. Looking closely, I saw several little figures dressed in brown peering through the bushes. They remained quiet for a few minutes and then disappeared. In a few seconds a dozen or more small people, about two feet in height, in bright clothes and with radiant faces, ran on to the lawn, dancing hither and thither. I glanced at Turvey to see if he saw anything, and whispered, 'Do you see them?' He nodded. These fairies played about, gradually approaching the hut. One little fellow, bolder than the others, came to a croquet hoop close to the hut and, using the hoop as a horizontal bar, turned round and round it, much to our amusement. Some of the others watched him, while others danced about, not in any set dance, but seemingly moving in sheer joy. This continued for four or five minutes, when suddenly, evidently in response to some signal or warning from those dressed in brown, who had remained at the edge of the lawn, they all ran into the wood. Just then a maid appeared coming from the house with tea. Never was tea so unwelcome, as evidently its appearance was the cause of the disappearance of our little visitors." Mr. Lonsdale adds, "I have seen fairies several times in the New Forest, but never so clearly as this." Here also the scene is laid in the heat of a summer day, and the division of the fairies into two different sorts remarkably borne out by the general descriptions.

Knowing Mr. Lonsdale as I do to be a responsible, well-balanced, and honourable man, I find such evidence as this very hard to put to one side. Here at least the sunstroke hypothesis is negatived, since both men sat in the shade of the hut and corroborated the observation of the other. On the other hand, each of the men, like Mr. Tweedale, was supernormal in psychic development, so that it might well happen that the maid for example, would not have seen the fairies, even if she had arrived earlier upon the scene.

I know a gentleman belonging to one of the learned professions whose career as, let us say, a surgeon would not be helped if this article were to connect him with fairy lore. As a matter of fact, in spite of his solemn avocations and his practical and virile character, he seems to be endowed with that faculty—let us call it the appreciation of higher vibrations—which opens up so wonderful a door to its possessor. He claims, or rather he admits, for he is reticent upon the subject, that he has carried this power of perception on from childhood, and his surprise is not so much at what he sees as at the failure of others to see the same thing. To show that it is not subjective, he tells the story that on one occasion, while traversing a field, he saw a little creature which beckoned eagerly that he should follow. He did so, and presently saw his guide pointing with an air of importance to the ground. There, between the furrows, lay a flint arrow-head which he carried home with him as a souvenir of the adventure.

Another friend of mine who claims to have the power of seeing fairies is Mr. Tom Tyrrell, the famous medium, whose clairvoyance and general psychic gifts are of the strongest character. I cannot easily forget how one evening in a Yorkshire hotel a storm of raps, sounding very much as if someone were cracking their fingers and thumb, broke out around his head, and how with his coffee-cup in one hand he flapped vigorously with the other to warn off his inopportune visitors. In answer to my question about fairies he says: "Yes, I do see these little pixies or fairies. I have seen them scores of times. But only in the woods and when I do a little fasting. They are a very real presence to me. What are they? I cannot say. I can never get nearer to the beggars than four or five yards. They seem afraid of me, and then scamper off up the trees like squirrels. I dare say if I were to go in the woods oftener I would perhaps gain their confidence more. They are certainly like human beings, only very small, say about twelve or fifteen inches high. I have noticed they are brown in colour, with fairly large heads and standing-up ears, out of proportion to the size of their bodies, and bandy legs. I am speaking of what I see. I have never come across any other clairvoyant who has seen them, though I have read that many do so. Probably they have something to do with Nature processes. The males have very short hair, and the females have rather long, straight hair."

The idea that these little creatures are occupied in consciously furthering Nature's projects—very much, I suppose, as the bee carries pollen—is repeated by the learned Dr. Vanstone, who combines great knowledge of theory with some considerable experience, though a high development of intellect is, in spite of Swedenborg's example, a bar to psychic perception. This would show, if it is correct, that we may have to return to the classical conception of something in the nature of naiads and fauns and spirits of the trees and groves. Dr. Vanstone, whose experiences are on the borderland between what is objective and what is sensed without being actually seen, writes to me: "I have been distinctly aware of minute intelligent beings in connection with the evolution of plant forces, particularly in certain localities; for instance, in Ecclesbourne Glen. Pond life yields to me the largest and best sense of fairy life, and not the floral world. I may be only clothing my subjective consciousness with unreal objective imaginations, but they are real to me as sentient, intelligent beings, able to communicate with us in varying distinctness. I am inclined to think that elemental beings are engaged, like factory hands, in facilitating the operation of Nature's laws."

Another gentleman who claims to have this most remarkable gift is Mr. Tom Charman, who builds for himself a shelter in the New Forest and hunts for fairies as an entomologist would for butterflies. In answer to my inquiries, he tells me that the power of vision came to him in childhood, but left him for many years, varying in proportion with his own nearness to Nature. According to this seer, the creatures are of many sizes, varying from a few inches to several feet. They are male, female, and children. He has not heard them utter sounds, but believes that they do so, of finer quality than we can hear. They are visible by night as well as by day, and show small lights about the same size as glow worms. They dress in all sorts of ways. Such is Mr. Charman's account.

It is, of course, easy for us who respond only to the more material vibrations to declare that all these seers are self-deluded, or are the victims of some mental twist. It is difficult for them to defend themselves from such a charge. It is, however, to be urged upon the other side that these numerous testimonies come from people who are very solid and practical and successful in the affairs of life. One is a distinguished writer, another an ophthalmic authority, a third a successful professional man, a fourth a lady engaged on public service, and so on. To waive aside the evidence of such people on the ground that it does not correspond with our own experience is an act of mental arrogance which no wise man will commit.

It is interesting to compare these various contemporary and first-hand accounts of the impressions which all these witnesses have received. I have already pointed out that the higher vibrations which we associate with hot sunshine, and which we actually seem to see in the shimmers of noontide, is associated with many of the episodes. Apart from this it must be admitted that the evidence is on the whole irregular. We have creatures described which range from five inches to two and a half feet. An advocate of the fairies might say that, since the tradition has always been that they procreate as human beings do, we are dealing with them in every stage of growth, which accounts for the varying size.

It seems to me, however, that a better case could be made out if it were pleaded that there have always been many different races of fairyland, and that samples of these races may greatly differ from each other, and may inhabit varying spots; so that an observer like Mr. Tyrrell, for example, may always have seen woodland elves, which bear no resemblance to gnomes or goblins. The monkey-like, brown-clad creatures of my professional friend, which were over two feet high, compare very closely with the creatures which little Baring-Gould saw climbing on to the horses. In both cases these taller fairies were reported from flat, plain-like locations; while the little old-man type varies completely from the dancing little feminine elf so beloved by Shakespeare. In the experience of Mr. Turvey and Mr. Lonsdale, two different types engaged in different tasks were actually seen at the same moment, the one being bright-coloured dancing elves, while the other were the brown-coloured attendants who guarded them.

The claim that the fairy rings so often seen in meadow or marshland are caused by the beat of fairy feet is certainly untenable, as they unquestionably come from fungi such as *Agaricus gambosus* or *Marasmius oreades*, which grow from a centre, continually deserting the exhausted ground, and spreading to that which is fresh. In this way a complete circle is formed, which may be quite small or may be of twelve-foot diameter. These circles appear just as often in woods from the same cause, but are smothered over by the decayed leaves among which the fungi grow. But though the fairies most certainly do not produce the rings, it might be asserted, and could not be denied, that the rings once formed, whatever their cause, would offer a very charming course for a circular ring-a-ring dance. Certainly from all time these circles have been associated with the gambols of the little people.

After these modern instances one is inclined to read with a little more gravity the account which our ancestors gave of these creatures; for, however fanciful in parts, it still may have had some core of truth. I say "our ancestors," but as a matter of fact there are shepherds on the South Downs to this day who will throw a bit of their bread and cheese over their shoulders at dinner-time for the little folks to consume. All over the United Kingdom, and especially in Wales and Ireland, the belief is largely held among those folks who are nearest to Nature. First of all it was always supposed that they lived within the earth. This was natural enough, since a sudden disappearance of a solid body could only be understood in that way. On the whole, their description was not grotesque, and fits easily into its place amid the examples already given. "They were of small stature," says one Welsh authority, quoted in Mrs. Lewes's *Stranger than Fiction*, "towards two feet in height, and their horses of the size of hares. Their clothes were generally white, but on certain occasions they have been seen dressed in green. Their gait was lively, and ardent and loving was their glance. . . . They were peaceful and kindly among themselves, diverting in their tricks, and charming in their walk and dancing." This mention of horses is somewhat out of the picture, but all the rest seems corroborative of what has already been stated.

One of the best of the ancient accounts is that of the Rev. R. Kirk, who occupied a parish at Monteith, on the edge of the Highlands, and wrote a pamphlet called *The Secret Commonwealth*, about the year 1680. He had very clear and definite ideas about these little creatures, and he was by no means a visionary, but a man of considerable parts, who was chosen afterwards to translate the Bible into Erse. His information about fairies tallies very well with that of the Welshman quoted above. He slips up in imagining that flint arrow-heads are indeed "fairy-bolts," but otherwise his contentions agree very well with our modern instances. They have tribes and orders, according to this Scottish clergyman. They eat. They converse in a thin, whistling sort of language. They have children, deaths, and burials. They are fond of frolic dancing. They have a regular state and polity, with rulers, laws, quarrels, and even battles. They are irresponsible creatures, not hostile to the human race unless they have reason to be angry, but even inclined to be helpful, since some of them, the brownies, are, by universal tradition, ready to aid in the household work if the family has known how to engage their affection.

An exactly similar account comes from Ireland, though the little folk seem to have imbibed the spirit of the island to the extent of being more mercurial and irascible. There are many cases on record where they are claimed to have shown their power, and to have taken revenge for some slight. In the *Larne Reporter* of March 31, 1866, as quoted in *True Irish Ghost Stories*, there is an account of how a stone which the fairies claimed having been built into a house, the inhabitants were bombarded with stones by invisible assailants by day and night, the missiles hurting no one, but causing great annoyance. These stories of stone-throwing are so common, and present such similar well-attested features in cases coming from every part of the world, that they may be accepted as a recognized preternatural phenomenon, whether it be the fairies or some other form of mischievous psychic force which caused the bombardment. The volume already quoted gives another remarkable case, where a farmer, having built a house upon what was really a fairy right-of-way between two "raths," or fairy mounds, was exposed to such persecution by noises and other disturbances that his family was at last driven out, and had to take refuge in the smaller house which they had previously occupied. This story is narrated by a correspondent from Wexford, who says that he examined the facts himself, examined the deserted home, cross-examined the owner, and satisfied himself that there were two raths in the vicinity, and that the house was in a dead-line between them.

I have particulars of a case in West Sussex which is analogous, and which I have been able to trace to the very lady to whom it happened. This lady desired to make a rock-garden, and for this purpose got some large boulders from a field hard by, which had always been known as the pixie stones, and built them into her new rockery. One summer evening this lady saw a tiny grey woman sitting on one of the boulders. The little creature slipped away when she knew that she had been observed. Several times she appeared upon the stones. Later the people in the village asked if the stones might be moved back to the field, "as," they said, "they are the pixie stones, and if they are removed from their place, misfortunes will happen to the village." The stones were restored.

But supposing that they actually do exist, what *are* these creatures? That is a subject upon which we can speculate only with more or less plausibility. Mr. David Gow, editor of *Light*, and a considerable authority upon psychic matters, had first formed the opinion that they were simply ordinary human spirits, seen, as it were, at the wrong end of a clairvoyant telescope, and therefore very minute. A study of the detailed accounts of their varied experience caused him to alter his view, and to conclude that they are really life forms which have developed along some separate line of evolution, and which for some morphological reason have assumed human shape in the strange way in which Nature reproduces her types like the figures on the mandrake root or the frost ferns upon the window.

In a remarkable book, *A Wanderer in the Spirit Lands*, published in 1896, the author, Mr. Farnese, under inspiration gives an account of many mysteries, including that of fairies. What he says fits in very closely with the facts that have been put forward, and goes beyond them. He says, speaking of elementals: "Some are in appearance like the gnomes and elves who are said to inhabit mountain caverns. Such, too, are the fairies whom men have seen in lonely and secluded places. Some of these beings are of a very low order of life, almost like the higher order of plants, save that they possess independent motion. Others are very lively and full of grotesque, unmeaning tricks. . . . As nations advance and grow more spiritual these lower forms of life die out from the astral plane of that earth's sphere, and succeeding generations begin at first to doubt and then to deny that they ever had any existence." This is one plausible way of explaining the disappearance of the faun, the dryad, the naiad, and all the creatures which are alluded to with such familiarity in the classics of Greece and Rome.

One may well ask what connection has this fairy-lore with the general scheme of psychic philosophy? The connection is slight and indirect, consisting only in the fact that anything which widens our conceptions of the possible, and shakes us out of our time-rutted lines of thought, helps us to regain our elasticity of mind, and thus to be more open to new philosophies. The fairy question is infinitely small and unimportant compared to the question of our own fate and that of the whole human race. The evidence also is very much less impressive, though, as I trust I have shown, it is not entirely negligible. These creatures are in any case remote from us, and their existence is of little more real importance than that of strange animals or plants. At the same time the perennial mystery why so many "flowers are born to blush unseen," and why Nature should be so lavish with gifts which human beings cannot use, would be solved if we understood that there were other orders of being which used the same earth and shared its blessings. It is at the lowest an interesting speculation which gives an added charm to the silence of the woods and the wildnerness of the moorland.

CHAPTER VII

Some Subsequent Cases

From the foregoing chapter it will be clear that there was a good deal of evidence which cannot easily be brushed aside as to the existence of these little creatures before the discovery of the photographs. These various witnesses have nothing to gain by their testimony, and it is not tainted by any mercenary consideration. The same remark applies to a number of cases which were communicated to me after the appearance of the articles in the *Strand*. One or two were more or less ingenious practical jokes, but from the others I have selected some which appear to be altogether reliable.

The gentleman whom I have already quoted under the name of Lancaster—he who was so doubtful as to the validity of the photographs—is himself a seer. He says:

"Personally I should describe fairies as being about 2 feet 6 inches to 3 feet in height, and dressed in duffle brown clothes. The nearest approach I can get to them is to say that they are spiritual monkeys. They have the active brains of monkeys, and their general instinct is to avoid mankind, but they are capable individually of becoming extremely attached to humans—or a human—but at any time they may bite you, like a monkey, and repent immediately afterwards. They have thousands of years of collective experience, call it 'inherited memory' if you like, but no reasoning faculties. They are just Peter Pans—children who never grow up.

"I remember asking one of our spirit group how one could get into touch with the brownies. He replied that when you could go into the woods and call the brown rabbits to you the other brownies will also come to you. Speaking generally, I should imagine that anyone who has had any truck with fairies must have obeyed the scriptural injunction to 'become as a little child,' i.e. he or she must be either simple or a Buddha."

This last phrase is a striking one, and it is curiously confirmed by a gentleman named Matthews, writing on January 3, 1921, from San Antonio, Texas. He declared that his three daughters, now married women, could all see fairies before the age of puberty, but never after it. The fairies said to them: "We are not of the human evolution. Very few humans have ever visited us. Only old souls well advanced in evolution or in a state of sex innocence can come to us." This repeats independently the idea of Mr. Lancaster.

These children seem to have gone into a trance state before they found themselves in the country of the fairies—a country of intelligent beings, very small, 12 to 18 inches high. According to their accounts, they were invited to attend banquets or celebrations, excursions on beautiful lakes, etc. Each child was able to entrance instantly. This they always did when they visited Fairyland, but when the fairies came to them, which was generally in the twilight, they sat in chairs in normal state watching them dance. The father adds: "My own children learned in this way to dance, so that at local entertainments audiences were delighted, though they never knew from what source they learned."

My correspondent does not say whether there is a marked difference between the European and the American type of fairy. No doubt, if these results are confirmed and followed up, there will be an exact classification in the future. If Bishop Leadbeater's clairvoyance can be trusted, there is, as will afterwards be shown, a very clear distinction between the elemental life of various countries, as well as many varieties in each particular country.

One remarkable first-hand case of seeing fairies came from the Rev. Arnold J. Holmes. He wrote:

"Being brought up in the Isle of Man one breathed the atmosphere of superstition (if you like to call it), the simple, beautiful faith of the Manx fisher folk, the childlike trust of the Manx girls, who to this day will not forget the bit of wood and coal put ready at the side of the fireplace in case the 'little people' call and need a fire. A good husband is the ultimate reward, and neglect in this respect a bad husband or no husband at all. The startling phenomena occurred on my journey home from Peel Town at night to St. Mark's (where I was Incumbent).

"After passing Sir Hall Caine's beautiful residence, Greeba Castle, my horse—a spirited one—suddenly stopped dead, and looking ahead I saw amid the obscure light and misty moon-beams what appeared to be a small army of indistinct figures—very small, clad in gossamer garments. They appeared to be perfectly happy, scampering and tripping along the road, having come from the direction of the beautiful sylvan glen of Greeba and St. Trinian's Roofless Church. The legend is that it has ever been the fairies' haunt, and when an attempt has been made on two occasions to put a roof on, the fairies have removed all the work during the night, and for a century no further attempts have been made. It has therefore been left to the 'little people' who claimed it as their own.

"I watched spellbound, my horse half mad with fear. The little happy army then turned in the direction of Witch's Hill, and mounted a mossy bank; one 'little man' of larger stature than the rest, about 14 inches high, stood at attention until all had passed him dancing, singing, with happy abandon, across the Valley fields towards St. John's Mount."

The wide distribution of the fairies may be judged by the following extremely interesting narrative from Mrs. Hardy, the wife of a settler in the Maori districts of New Zealand:

"After reading about what others have seen I am encouraged to give you an experience of my own, which happened about five years ago. Will you please excuse my mentioning a few domestic details connected with the story? Our home is built on the top of a ridge. The ground was levelled for some distance to allow for sites for the house, buildings, lawns, etc. The ground on either side slopes steeply down to an orchard on the left, and shrubbery and paddock on the right, bounded by the main road. One evening when it was getting dusk I went into the yard to hang the tea-towels on the clothes-line. As I stepped off the verandah, I heard a sound of soft galloping coming from the direction of the orchard. I thought I must be mistaken, and that the sound came from the road, where the Maoris often gallop their horses. I crossed the yard to get the pegs, and heard the galloping coming nearer. I walked to the clothes-line, and stood under it with my arms uplifted to peg the towel on the line, when I was aware of the galloping close behind me, and suddenly a little figure, riding a tiny pony, rode right under my uplifted arms. I looked round, to see that I was surrounded by eight or ten tiny figures on tiny ponies like dwarf Shetlands. The little figure who came so close to me stood out quite clearly in the light that came from the window, but he had his back to it, and I could not see his face. The faces of the others were quite brown, also the ponies were brown. If they wore clothes they were close-fitting like a child's jersey suit. They were like tiny dwarfs, or children of about two years of age. I was very startled, and called out, 'Goodness! what is this?' I think I must have frightened them, for at the sound of my voice they all rode through the rose trellis across the drive, and down the shubbery. I heard the soft galloping dying away into the distance, and listened until the sound was gone, then went into the house. My daughter, who has had several psychic experiences, said to me: 'Mother, how white and startled you look! What have you seen? And who were you speaking to just now in the yard?' I said, 'I have seen the fairies ride!' "

The little fairy horses are mentioned by several writers, and yet it must be admitted that their presence makes the whole situation far more complicated and difficult to understand. If horses, why not dogs? And we find ourselves in a whole new world upon the fairy scale. I have convinced myself that there is overwhelming evidence for the fairies, but I have by no means been able to assure myself of these adjuncts.

The following letter from a young lady in Canada, daughter of one of the leading citizens of Montreal, and personally known to me, is interesting on account of the enclosed photograph here reproduced. She says:

"The enclosed photograph was taken this summer at Waterville, New Hampshire, with a 2A Brownie camera (portrait lens attached) by Alverda, eleven years old. The father is able, clear headed, enthusiastic on golf and billiards; the mother on Japanese art; neither interested in psychic matters much. The child has been frail and imaginative, but sweet and incapable of deceit.

"The mother tells me she was with the child when the picture was taken. The mushrooms pleased the little girl, and she knelt down and photographed them. As an indication of their ordinary size, they are *Amainta muscaria*.

"There was no such figure to be seen as appears in the picture.

"There was no double exposure. The picture astonished them when developed. The parents guarantee its honesty, but are mystified.

"Do you think shadows, etc., can explain it? I think the line of the right shoulder and arm especially are too decisive to be thus brushed away."

I rather agree with the writer, but it is a point which each reader can decide for himself upon examination of the photograph. It is certainly very vague after the Yorkshire examples.

New Zealand would appear to be quite a fairy centre, for I have another letter from a lady in those beautiful islands, which is hardly less interesting and definite than the one already quoted. She says:

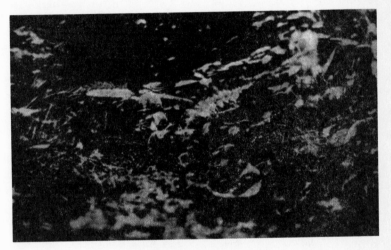

The photograph from Canada.

"I have seen fairies in all parts of New Zealand, but especially in the fern-clad gullies of the North Island. Most of my unfoldment for mediumship was carried out in Auckland, and during that time I spent hours in my garden, and saw the fairies most often in the evening just after sunset. From observation I notice they usually lived or else appeared about the perennial plants. I saw brown fairies and green fairies, and they all had wings of a filmy appearance. I used to talk to them and ask them to make special pet plants and cuttings I put in the garden grow well, and I am sure they did, by the results I got. Since I came to Sydney, I have also seen the green fairies. I tried an experiment last spring. I had some pheasant-eye narcissus growing in the garden. I saw the green fairies about them. I transplanted one of the bulbs to a pot when half grown, and took it with me when I went away for a short holiday. I asked the fairies to keep it growing. I watched it closely every evening—a green-clad fairy, sometimes two or three of them, would appear on the pot under the plant and whatever they did to it during the night I do not know, but next morning it was very much bigger, and, although transplanted, etc., it flowered three weeks before those in the garden. I am now living at Rochdale, Sydney, with friends both Australians and Spiritualists, and they also have seen the fairies from childhood up. I am sure animals see them. The fairies appear every evening in a little wild corner of the garden we leave for them, and our cat sits and watches them intently, but never attempts to spring at them as he does at other moving objects. If you care to make use of the information contained in this letter, you are welcome to do so."

I had another interesting letter from Mrs. Roberts, of Dunedin, one of the most gifted women in psychic matters whom I met during my Australian wanderings, in which she describes, as the last writer has done, the intimate connection between these elemental forms of life and the flowers, asserting that she has continually seen them tending the plants in her own garden.

From Ireland I received several fairy stories which seemed to be honestly told, even if some margin must be left for errors of observation. One of these seems to link up the fairy kingdom with spiritual communication, for the writer, Miss Winter, of Blarney, in Cork, says:

"We received communications from a fairy named Bebel several times, one of them lasting nearly an hour. The communication was as decided and swift as from the most powerful spirit. He told us that he was a Leprechaun (male), but that in a ruined fort near us dwelt the Pixies. Our demesne had been the habitation of Leprechauns always, and they with their Queen Picel, mounted on her gorgeous dragon-fly, found all they required in our grounds.

"He asked most lovingly about my little grandchildren, who visit us frequently, and since then he has been in the habit of communicating with them, when we have yielded the table to them entirely, and just listened to the pure fun he and they were having together. He told them that the fairies find it quite easy to talk to the rabbits, and that they disliked the dogs because they chased them. They have great fun with the hens, on whose backs they ride, but they do not like them because they 'jeer' at them. When he mentioned the old fort, I thought he referred to Blarney Castle, not far away, but on relating the incident to a farmer's daughter, whose family has been in the neighbourhood for a very long time, she informed me that a labourer's cottage at the entrance to our avenue is built on the site of an old fort, information absolutely new to us."

A few more may be added to my list of witnesses, which might be greatly extended. Miss Hall, of Bristol, writes:

"I, too, have seen fairies, but never until now have I dared to mention it for fear of ridicule. It was many years ago. I was quite a child of six or seven years, and then, as now, passionately fond of all flowers, which always seem to me living creatures. I was seated in the middle of a road in some cornfields, playing with a group of poppies, and never shall I forget my utter astonishment at seeing a funny little man playing hide-and-seek among these flowers to amuse me, as I thought. He was quick as a dart. I watched him for quite a long time, then he disappeared. He seemed a merry little fellow, but I cannot ever remember his face. In colour he was a sage-green, his limbs were round and had the appearance of geranium stalks. He did not seem to be clothed, and was about three inches high and slender. I often looked for him again, but without success."

Mr. J. Foot Young, the well-known water diviner, writes:

"Some years ago I was one of a party invited to spend the afternoon on the lovely slopes of Oxeford Hill, in the county of Dorset. The absence of both trees and hedges in this locality enables one to see without obstruction for long distances. I was walking with my companion, who lives in the locality, some little distance from the main party, when to my astonishment I saw a number of what I thought to be very small children, about a score in number, and all dressed in little gaily-coloured short skirts, their legs being bare. Their hands were joined, and all held up, as they merrily danced round in a perfect circle. We stood watching them, when in an instant they all vanished from our sight. My companion told me they were fairies, and that they often came to that particular part to hold their revels. It may be our presence disturbed them."

Mrs. Ethel Enid Wilson, of Worthing, writes:

"I quite believe in fairies. Of course, they are really nature spirits. I have often seen them on fine sunny days playing in the sea, and riding on the waves, but no one I have ever been with at the time has been able to see them, excepting once my little nephews and nieces saw them too. They were like little dolls, quite small, with beautiful bright hair, and they were constantly moving and dancing about."

Mrs. Rose, of Southend-on-Sea, told us in a chat on the subject:

"I think I have always seen fairies. I see them constantly here in the shrubbery by the sea. They congregate under the trees and float around about the trees, and gnomes come around to protect them. The gnomes are like little old men, with little green caps, and their clothes are generally neutral green. The fairies themselves are in light draperies. I have also seen them in the conservatory of my house, floating about among the flowers and plants. The fairies appear to be perpetually playing, excepting when they go to rest on the turf or in a tree, and I once saw a group of gnomes standing on each others' shoulders, like gymnasts on the stage. They seemed to be living as much as I am. It is not imagination. I have seen the gnomes arranging a sort of moss bed for the fairies, just like a mother-bird putting her chicks to bed. I don't hear any sounds from the gnomes or fairies, but they always look happy, as if they were having a real good time."

Miss Eva Longbottom, L.R.A.M., A.R.C.M., of Bristol, a charming vocalist, who has been blind from birth, told us in an interview:

"I have seen many fairies with my mind's eyes (that is, clairvoyantly). They are of various kinds, the ones I see. The music fairies are very beautiful. 'Argent' describes them, for they make you think of silver, and they have dulcet silvery voices. They speak and sing, but more in sound than in distinct words—a language of their own, a fairy tongue. Their music is a thing we cannot translate. It exists in itself. I don't think Mendelssohn has truly caught it, but Mr. Coleridge-Taylor's music reminds me of the music I have heard from the fairies themselves; his fairy ballads are very charming.

"Then there are dancing fairies. Their dancing is dainty and full of grace, a sweet old style of dance, without any tangles in it. I am generally alone when I see them, not necessarily in a woodland, but wherever the atmosphere is poetical. They are quite real.

"Another kind is the poem fairies. They are more ethereal, and of a violet shade. If you could imagine Perdita in the *Midsummer*

Night's Dream, translated from the stage into a real fairy, you would have a good idea of the poem fairy. She has a very beautiful girlish character. The same might be said of Miranda, but she is more sentimental.

"The colour fairies are also most interesting. If you can imagine each colour transformed into a fairy you may get an idea of what they are like. They are in airy forms and dance and sing in the tone of their colours. I have not seen any brownies, as I do not take so much interest in the domestic side of the fairies' life.

"When I was young I had it so much impressed on me that fairies were imaginary beings that I would not believe in them, but when I was about fourteen I began to realize them, and now I love them. Perhaps it was the deeper study of the arts that brought them to me. I have felt a sympathetic vibration for them and they have made me feel that we were friends. I have had a great deal of happiness and good fortune in my life, and perhaps I can attribute some of that to the fairies."

These last examples I owe to Mr. John Lewis, Editor of the *Psychic Gazette,* who collected them. I think I may fairly claim that if all of them be added to those which I have quoted in my original article, and these again be linked up with the Cottingley children and photographs, we are in a position to present our case with some confidence to the public.

CHAPTER VIII

The Theosophic View of Fairies

Of all religions and philosophies in Western lands I know none save that ancient teaching now called Theosophy which has any place in it for elemental forms of life. Therefore, since we have established some sort of independent case for their existence, it is well that we should examine carefully what they teach and see how far it fits in with what we have been able to gather or to demonstrate.

There is no one who has a better right to speak upon the point than my co-worker, Mr. E. L. Gardner, since he is both the discoverer of the fairies and a considerable authority upon theosophic teaching. I am glad, therefore, to be able to include some notes from his pen.

"For the most part," he writes, "amid the busy commercialism of modern times, the fact of their existence has faded to a shadow, and a most delightful and charming field of nature study has too long been veiled. In this twentieth century there is promise of the world stepping out of some of its darker shadows. Maybe it is an indication that we are reaching the silver lining of the clouds when we find ourselves suddenly presented with actual photographs of these enchanting little creatures—relegated long since to the realm of the imaginary and fanciful.

"Now, what *are* the fairies?

"First, it must be clearly understood that all that *can* be photographed must of necessity be physical. Nothing of a subtler order could in the nature of things affect the sensitive plate. So-called spirit photographs, for instance, imply necessarily a certain degree of materialization before the 'form' could come within the range even of the most sensitive of films. But well within our physical octave there are degrees of density that elude ordinary vision. Just as there are many stars in the heavens recorded by the camera that no human eye has ever seen directly, so there is a vast array of living creatures, whose bodies are of that rare tenuity and subtlety from our point of view that they lie beyond the range of our normal senses. Many children and sensitives see them, and hence our fairy lore—all founded on actual and now demonstrable fact!

"Fairies use bodies of a density that we should describe, in non-technical language, as of a lighter than gaseous nature, but we should be entirely wrong if we thought them in consequence unsubstantial. In their own way they are as real as we are, and perform functions in connection with plant life of an important and most fascinating character. To hint at one phase—many a reader will have remarked on the lasting freshness and beauty of flowers cut and tended by one person, and, on the other hand, their comparatively short life when in the care of another. The explanation is to be found in the kindly devotion of the one person and the comparative indifference of the other, which emotions affect keenly the nature spirits in whose immediate care the flowers are. Their response to love and tenderness is quickly evidenced in their charges.

"Fairies are not born and do not die as we do, though they have their periods of outer activity and retirement. Allied to the *lepidoptera*, or butterfly genus, of our familiar acquaintance rather than to the mammalian line, they partake of certain characteristics that are obvious. There is little or no mentality awake—simply a gladsome, irresponsible joyousness of life that is abundantly in evidence in their enchanting abandon. The diminutive human form, so widely assumed, is doubtless due, at least in a great measure, to the powerful influence of human thought, the strongest creative power in our cycle.

"In the investigations I have pursued in Yorkshire, the New Forest, and Scotland, many fairy lovers and observers have been interviewed and their accounts compared. In most cases I was interested to note that my share in making public the photographs of Cottingley was the worst sort of introduction imaginable. Few fairy lovers have looked with favour on that. Reproaches have been frequent and couched in no measured terms, for the photographs have been resented as an unwarranted intrusion and desecration. Only after earnest assurances as to my own attitude could I get farther and obtain those intimate confidences that I have compared and checked and pieced together and am at liberty to narrate here.

"The function of the nature spirit of woodland, meadow, and garden, indeed in connection with vegetation generally, is to furnish the vital connecting link between the stimulating energy, of the sun and the raw material of the form. That growth of a plant which we regard as the customary and inevitable result of associating the three factors of sun, seed, and soil would never take place if the fairy builders were absent. We do not obtain music from an organ by associating the wind, a composer's score, and the instrument—the vital link supplied by the organist, though he may be unseen, is needed—and similarly the nature spirits are essential to the production of the plant.

"THE FAIRY BODY.—The normal working body of the gnome and fairy is not of human nor of any other definite form, and herein lies the explanation of much that has been puzzling concerning the nature-spirit kingdom generally. They have no clean-cut shape normally, and one can only describe them as small, hazy, and somewhat luminous clouds of colour with a brighter spark-like nucleus. As such they cannot be defined in terms of form any more than one can so describe a tongue of flame. In such a body they fill their office, working *inside* the plant structure. 'Magnetic' is the only word that can describe their method. Instantly responsive to stimulus, they appear to be influenced from two directions—the physical outer conditions prevailing and an inner intelligent urge. These two influences determine their working activity. Some, and these are by far the most numerous, work on cell construction and organization, and are comparatively small when assuming the human form, being two to three inches high. Others are concerned exclusively with root development below ground, while others are apparently specialists in colour and 'paint' the flowers by means of the streaming motion of their cloudlike bodies. There appears to be little trace of any selective or discriminating work done individually. They all seem actuated by a common influence that affects them continuously, and which strongly suggests the same type of instinctive prompting that marks the bee and ant.

"THE HUMAN FORM.—Though the nature spirit must be regarded as practically irresponsible, living a gladsome, joyous, and delightfully untrammelled life, each member appears to possess at least a temporary definite individuality at times, and to rejoice in it. The diminutive human form—sometimes grotesque, as in the case of brownie and gnome, sometimes beautifully graceful, as in the surface fairy variety—if conditions allow, is assumed in a flash. For a while it is retained, and it seems clear that the definite and comparatively concrete shape affords pleasure above the ordinary. There is no organization perceptible, as one might perhaps hastily infer. The content of the body still appears homogeneous, though somewhat denser, and the shape of 'human' is usually only seen when not at work. The nature spirit so clothed indulges in active movement in skipping and dancing gestures and exhibits a gay abandon suggestive of the keenest delight in the experience. It is evidently 'time off' and play for it, though its work seems charming enough. If disturbed or alarmed the change back to the slightly subtler vehicle, the magnetic cloud, is as sudden as the birth. What determines the shape assumed and how the transformation is effected is not clear. One may speculate as to the influence of human thought, individual or in the mass, and quite probably the explanation when found will include this influence as a factor—but I am intent here not on theorizing, but on a narrative of observed happenings. One thing is clear—the nature-spirit form is objective—objective, that is, in the sense in which we apply that term to a stone, a tree, and a human body.

'FAIRY WINGS.—The wings are a feature that one would hardly expect to find in conjunction with arms. In this respect the insect type, with its several limbs and two or more wings, is a nearer model. But there is no articulation and no venation, and moreover the wings are not used for flying. 'Streaming emanations' is the only description one can apply. In some varieties, particularly the sylphs, the streamers surround the body, as by a luminous aura sprayed to a feathery mist. I was told that the earlier and more elaborate Red Indian head-dresses must have been inspired from this source, so suggestive are they, though the best of them are but poor copies of the originals.

"FOOD.—There is no food taken, as we should regard it. Nourishment, usually abundant and ample for sustenance, is absorbed directly by a rhythmic breathing or pulse. Resource to the magnetic bath on occasion appears to be their only special restorative. The perfume of flowers is delighted in, and, reversely, disagreeable odours repel. This is one of many reasons, besides timidity, why human society is usually avoided, there being little that is inviting in that connection for them, and much that is obnoxious.

"BIRTH, DEATH, AND SEX.—Any estimate of length of life is misleading, because comparison with ourselves cannot be made. There is no real birth nor death, as we understand the terms— simply a gradual emergence from, and a return to, a subtler state of being. This process takes some time, probably years in certain varieties, and their life on the denser level, corresponding to our adult period, may be as long as the average human. There is nothing definite in all this, however, except the fact of the *gradual* emergence and return. There is no sex, as we should regard it, though, so far as I can gather, there is division and sub-division of 'body' at a much subtler and earlier level than that usually sensed. This process seems to correspond to the fission and budding of our familiar simple animalcules, with the addition, towards the end of the cycle, of fusion or reassembly into the larger unit.

"SPEECH AND GESTURE.—Below the sylph there appears to be nothing, or very little, in the way of a language of words. Communication is possible by inflexion and gesture, much as the same can be exercised with domestic animals. Indeed, the relation of human with the lower nature spirits seems to be about on a par with that of kittens, puppies, and birds. Yet there is abundant evidence of a tone language among them. Music by pipe and flute is common, though to the human ear of the quaintest character— but whether the instrument or the voice is the real source I cannot yet determine. The higher orders of nature spirits are adding mentality to the emotional development, and speech with them is possible. Their attitude to ordinary humanity is unfriendly rather than well disposed, and often hostile, arising probably from our utter disregard of the amenities. I am beginning, to see sense and reason in the 'burnt-offerings' of yore. Pollution of the atmosphere is a horror to the sylphs and deeply resented. An ancient saying I had seen somewhere came to mind when discussing the beautiful air-spirits and their work: 'Agni (Fire) is the mouth of the gods!' Our sanitary and burial customs are doubtless still capable of improvement! One fairy lover said to me gleefully, 'Ah, well! you! will never be able to get photographs of the sylphs—they know too much for you!' If we can establish friendly relations with them, though, the weather may be ours, if that be desirable!

"CAUSE AND EFFECT.—The dissection and examination of vegetable forms, however exhaustive, is but an analysis of *effects*. No adequate *cause* is therein to be found any more than a dissection of a sculpture will disclose the craftsman. The amazing skill in evidence in the plant kingdom in construction, adaptation, and adornment demand the labour of workman, mechanic, and artist. Their recognition in the nature spirits fills the vague hiatus between the sun's energy and the material wrought. On our own human side of the line the finding of two pieces of wood nailed together would unmistakably point to a workman of sorts, yet we are accustomed to gaze with wonder and admiration on the exquisitely built forms of a whole kingdom, and murmur 'evolutionary processes,' or 'the hand of God,' according to our temperament. An agent is necessary on the one side and no less on the other.

"MODE OF WORKING.—The feature that will appeal to every nature lover interested in the vital processes of plant life is the craftsmanship of the Nature-spirit agent. An inference, if it be simple enough, often escapes us, though in this case the experiences gathered of our own human labour suggest the analogy vividly. An analogy with a difference, however, for the hidden manner of work of the nature spirit is in most respects the exact opposite in character to our own. In this physical world we labour with hands and tools, and work consistently on exteriors, always indeed handling and applying our material from the outside. Addition, accretion, is our constructive method. We find ourselves made that way, and it is our characteristic mode of approach. The nature spirits operate from the interior, working from a centre outwards. Their aim appears to be to achieve an ever-closer touch with the environment, and to that end the driving urge of their activity is how best to adapt the means to their hand. It is easy to perceive the cause of variety in nature in view of this striving endeavour to organize the vehicle that the nature spirits use, and so gain in endless ways a closer touch. Flower colouring, mimicry, seed protection and distribution, defensive and aggressive measures, all the thousand-and-one devices employed to attain an end, point to an intelligence working through agents who, at their own level, are often in more or less antagonistic relation with each other. Variety and difference is as much in evidence as among humanity, and makes for that diversity of form and custom that we find on our side so fruitful of experience. In the tilling of the soil and the culture of plant life for our own purposes we have worked intimately together—though unconsciously. The efforts of nature spirits working by themselves *without* our assistance produce the wild flowers and berries of our woodlands and meadows, while partnership *with* the human yields a record of cultivated cereal, flower, and fruit, immensely richer.

"PLANT CONSCIOUSNESS.—The relation of the nature spirit to the consciousness functioning through the vegetable kingdom generally is an interesting study too, for the twain appear quite separate. This might perhaps be likened to the rôle respectively of crew and passenger in a ship. The slumbering, or at best slowly awakening, consciousness of the plant, makes of it little more than an idle traveller, whereas the nature spirits, alert and active, attend to the upkeep and navigation of the craft, and the voyage through the kingdom means a growth and development for both.

"THE FUTURE.—What might follow an intelligent understanding of the 'little people,' and the establishment of mutual good feeling, opens up a prospect alluring in the extreme. It would be for us a working in the light instead of in darkness. A foretaste of such co-operation may be gathered by noting the effect of a devoted lover of flowers on his or her charges. The nature spirit responds to emotion and appears keenly appreciative of kindly attention and affection. Whether this applies with any force to any but the varieties concerned with flowers and fruits I cannot say, but it certainly does to them, and the intelligent direction of effort in place of empirical incident tempts one's speculation to run riot as to future possibilities.

"The awakened self-consciousness of the human kingdom, with a vigorous mentality linked to kindly emotion and physical action, may enable an ages-old debt to be adjusted. We have served the nature-spirit line of evolution consciously not at all, but by understanding the situation we can co-operate together intelligently and helpfully, and the service of both to mutual advantage can take the place, of blind experiment and groping self-interest."—E. L. G.

In the literature of Theosophy, I know no one who treats the elemental forces of nature more fully than Bishop Leadbeater, whom I met in my Australian travels, and who impressed me by his venerable appearance, his ascetic habits, and his claims to a remarkable clairvoyancy which has, as he alleges, opened up many of the Arcana. In his book *The Hidden Side of Things* he talks very fully of the fairies of many lands.

Dealing with the little creatures whom so many of my

informants have seen tending flowers, the seer says:

"The little creatures that look after flowers may be divided into two great classes, though of course there are many varieties of each kind. The first class may properly be called elementals, for, beautiful though they are, they are in reality only thought-forms, and therefore they are not really living creatures at all. Perhaps I should rather say that they are only temporary living creatures, for, though they are very active and busy during their little lives, they have no real evolving, reincarnating life in them, and when they have done their work they just go to pieces and dissolve into the surrounding atmosphere, precisely as our own thought-forms do. They are the thought-forms of the Great Beings, or angels, who are in charge of the evolution of the vegetable kingdom.

"When one of these Great Ones has a new idea connected with one of the kinds of plants or flowers which are under his charge, he often creates a thought-form for the special purpose of carrying out that idea. It usually takes the form either of an etheric model of the flower itself or of a little creature which hangs round the plant or the flower all through the time that the buds are forming, and gradually builds them into the shape and colour of which the angel has thought. But as soon as the plant has fully grown, or the flower has opened, its work is over and its power is exhausted, and, as I have said, it just simply dissolves, because the will to do that piece of work was the only soul that it had.

"But there is quite another kind of little creature which is very frequently seen playing about with flowers, and this time it is a real nature spirit. There are many varieties of these also. One of the commonest forms is, as I have said, something very much like a humming-bird, and it may often be seen buzzing round the flowers much in the same way as a humming-bird or a bee does. These beautiful little creatures will never become human, because they are not in the same line of evolution as we are. The life which is now animating them has come up through grasses and cereals, such as wheat and oats, when it was in the vegetable kingdom, afterwards through ants and bees when it was in the animal kingdom. Now it has reached the level of these tiny nature spirits, and its next stage will be to ensoul some of the beautiful fairies with etheric bodies who live upon the surface of the earth. Later on they will become salamanders, or fire spirits, and later still they will become sylphs, or air spirits, having only astral bodies instead of etheric. Later still they will pass through the different stages of the great kingdom of the angels."

Speaking of the national characteristis of fairies, he says with all the assurance of an actual observer (page 97):

"No contrast could well be more marked than that between the vivacious, rollicking, orange-and-purple or scarlet-and-gold mannikins who dance among the vineyards of Sicily and the almost wistful grey-and-green creatures who move so much more sedately amidst the oaks and furze-covered heaths in Brittany, or the golden-brown 'good people' who haunt the hillsides of Scotland.

"In England the emerald-green kind is probably the commonest, and I have seen it also in the woods in France and Belgium, in far-away Massachusetts, and on the banks of the Niagara River. The vast plains of the Dakotas are inhabited by a black-and-white kind which I have not seen elsewhere, and California rejoices in a lovely white-and-gold species which also appears to be unique.

"In Australia the most frequent type is a very distinctive creature of a wonderful luminous sky-blue colour; but there is a wide diversity between the etheric inhabitants of New South Wales or Victoria and those of tropical Northern Queensland. These latter approximate closely to those of the Dutch Indies. Java seems specially prolific in these graceful creatures, and the kinds most common there are two distinct types, both monochromatic—one indigo blue with faint metallic gleamings, and the other a study in all known shades of yellow—quaint, but wonderfully effective and attractive.

"A striking local variety is gaudily ringed with alternate bars of green and yellow, like a football jersey. This ringed type is possibly a race peculiar to that part of the world, for I saw red and yellow similarly arranged in the Malay Peninsula, and green and white on the other side of the Straits in Sumatra. That huge island also rejoices in the possession of a lovely pale heliotrope tribe which I have seen before only in the hills of Ceylon. Down in New Zealand their speciality is a deep blue shot with silver, while in the South Sea Islands one meets with a silvery-white variety, which coruscates with all the colours of the rainbow, like a figure of mother-of-pearl.

"In India we find all sorts, from the delicate rose-and-pale-green, or pale-blue-and-primrose of the hill country to the rich medley of gorgeously gleaming colours, almost barbaric in their intensity and profusion, which is characteristic of the plains. In some parts of that marvellous country I have seen the black-and-gold type which is more usually associated with the African desert, and also a species which resembles a statuette made out of a gleaming crimson metal, such as was the orichalcum of the Atlanteans.

"Somewhat akin to this last is a curious variety which looks as though cast out of bronze and burnished; it appears to make its home in the immediate neighbourhood of volcanic disturbances, since the only places in which it has been seen so far are the slopes of Vesuvius and Etna, the interior of Java, the Sandwich Islands, the Yellowstone Park in North America, and a certain part of the North Island of New Zealand. Several indications seem to point to the conclusion that this is a survival of a primitive type, and represents a sort of intermediate stage between the gnome and the fairy.

"In some cases, districts close together are found to be inhabited by quite different classes of nature spirits; for example, as has already been mentioned, the emerald-green elves are common in Belgium, yet a hundred miles away in Holland hardly one of them is to be seen, and their place is taken by a sober-looking dark-purple species."

Very interesting indeed is his account of the Irish fairies.

Speaking of a sacred mountain in Ireland, he says:

"A curious fact is that altitude above the sea-level seems to affect their distribution, those who belong to the mountains scarcely ever, intermingling with those of the plains. I well remember, when climbing Slieve-na-mon, one of the traditionally sacred hills of Ireland, noticing the very definite lines of demarcation between the different types. The lower slopes, like the surrounding plains, were alive with the intensely active and mischievous little red-and-black race which swarms all over the south and west of Ireland, being especially attracted to the magnetic centres established nearly two thousand years ago by the magic-working priests of the old Milesian race to ensure and perpetuate their domination over the people by keeping them under the influence of the great illusion. After half an hour's climbing, however, not one of these red-and-black gentry was to be seen, but instead the hill-side was populous with the gentler blue-and-brown type which long ago owed special allegiance to the Tuatha-de-Danaan.

"These also had their zone and their well-defined limits, and no nature spirit of either type ever ventured to trespass upon the space round the summit, sacred to the great green angels who have watched there for more than two thousand years, guarding one of the centres of living force that link the past to the future of that mystic land of Erin. Taller far than the height of man, these giant forms, in colour like the first new leaves of spring, soft, luminous, shimmering, indescribable, look forth over the world with wondrous eyes that shine like stars, full of the peace of those who live in the eternal, waiting with the calm certainty of knowledge until the appointed time shall come. One realizes very fully the power and importane of the hidden side of things when one beholds such a spectacle as that."

For fuller information the reader may well be referred to the original, published by the Theosophical Publishing House. The book is a storehouse of knowledge upon all occult matters, and certainly the details concerning the fairies fit in remarkably well with the information from other sources.

I have now laid before the reader the full circumstances in connection with the five successful photographs taken at Cottingley. I have added the experience of a clairvoyant officer in the company of the girls upon the third and unsuccessful attempt to get photographs. I have analysed some of the criticism which we have had to meet. I have given the reader the opportunity of judging the evidence for a considerable number of alleged cases, collected before and after the Cottingley incident. Finally, I have placed before him the general theory of the place in creation of such creatures, as defined by the only system of thought which has found room for them. Having read and weighed all this, the investigator is in as strong a position as Mr. Gardner or myself, and each must give his own verdict. I do not myself contend that the proof is as overwhelming as in the case of spiritualistic phenomena. We cannot call upon the brightest brains in the scientific world, the Crookes, the Lodges, or the Lombrosos, for confirmation. But that also may come, and for the present, while more evidence will be welcome, there is enough already available to convince any reasonable man that the matter is not one which can be readily dismissed, but that a case actually exists which up to now has not been shaken in the least degree by any of the criticism directed against it. Far from being resented, such criticism, so long as it is earnest and honest, must be most welcome to those whose only aim is the fearless search for truth.